BABYMOUSE AND FRIENDS*

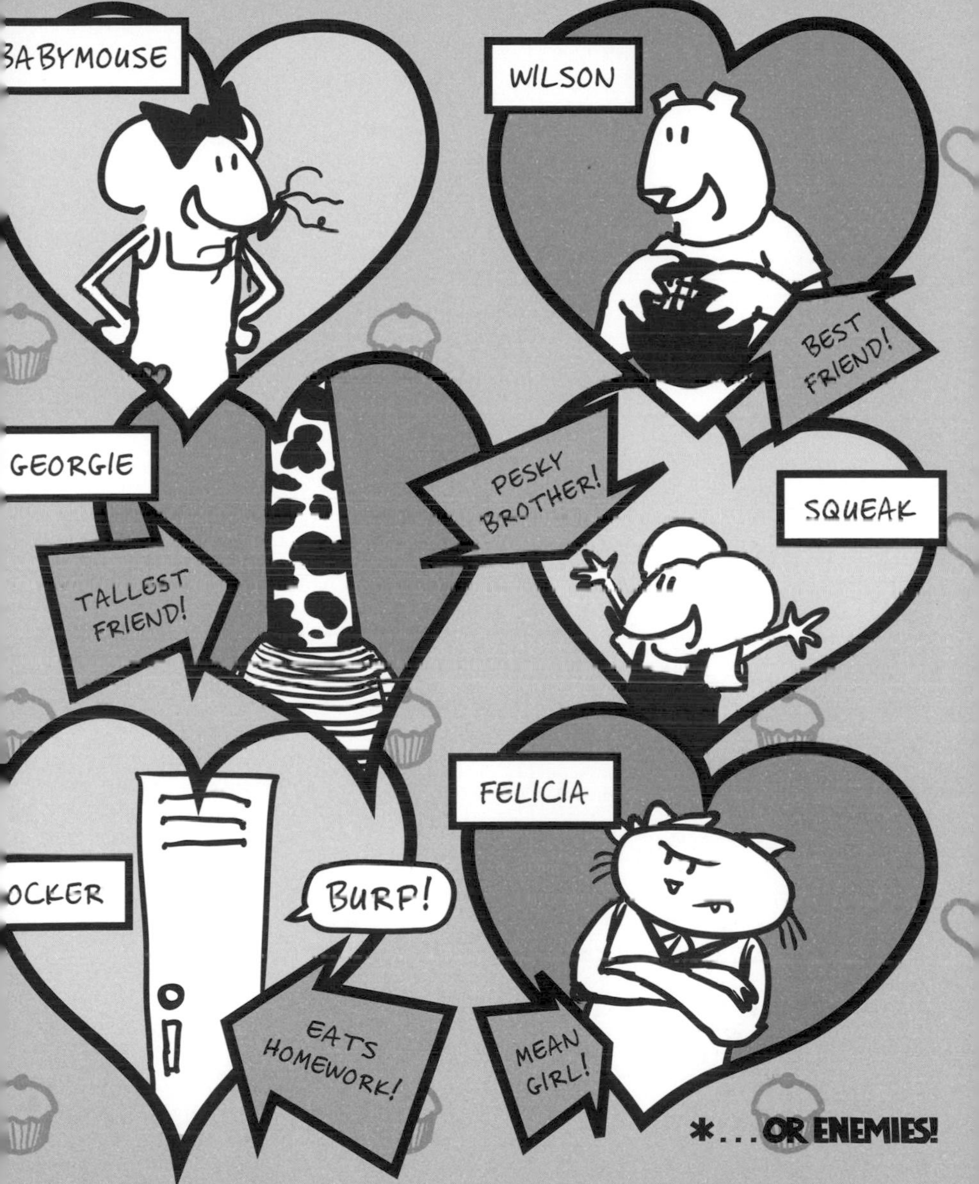
BABYMOUSE
WILSON
BEST FRIEND!
GEORGIE
PESKY BROTHER!
SQUEAK
TALLEST FRIEND!
LOCKER
BURP!
EATS HOMEWORK!
FELICIA
MEAN GIRL!

*. . . OR ENEMIES!

Be sure to read **ALL** the **BABYMOUSE** books:

#1 BABYMOUSE: Queen of the World!
#2 BABYMOUSE: Our Hero
#3 BABYMOUSE: Beach Babe
#4 BABYMOUSE: Rock Star
#5 BABYMOUSE: Heartbreaker
#6 CAMP BABYMOUSE
#7 BABYMOUSE: Skater Girl
#8 BABYMOUSE: Puppy Love
#9 BABYMOUSE: Monster Mash
#10 BABYMOUSE: The Musical
#11 BABYMOUSE: Dragonslayer
#12 BABYMOUSE: Burns Rubber
#13 BABYMOUSE: Cupcake Tycoon
#14 BABYMOUSE: Mad Scientist
#15 A Very BABYMOUSE Christmas
#16 BABYMOUSE for President
#17 Extreme BABYMOUSE
#18 Happy Birthday, BABYMOUSE
#19 BABYMOUSE: Bad Babysitter

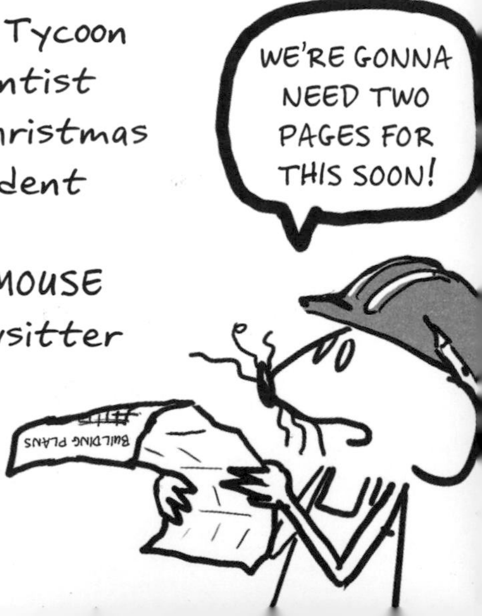
WE'RE GONNA NEED TWO PAGES FOR THIS SOON!
BUILDING PLANS

BABYMOUSE  BURNS RUBBER

BY JENNIFER L. HOLM & MATTHEW HOLM

RANDOM HOUSE NEW YORK

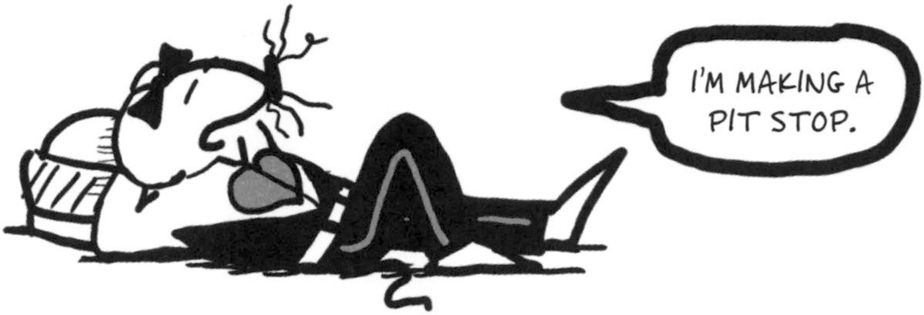
I'M MAKING A
PIT STOP.

This is a work of fiction. Names, characters, places, and incidents either are the product of the authors' imagination or are used fictitiously. Any resemblance to actual persons, living or dead, events, or locales is entirely coincidental.

Published in the United States by Random House Children's Books,
a division of Penguin Random House LLC, New York.

Random House and the colophon are registered trademarks of Penguin Random House LLC.

Visit us on the Web!
randomhousekids.com
Babymouse.com

Educators and librarians, for a variety of teaching tools, visit us at
RHTeachersLibrarians.com

Library of Congress Cataloging-in-Publication Data
Holm, Jennifer L.
Babymouse : burns rubber / by Jennifer and Matthew Holm. — 1st ed.
p. cm.
Summary: Babymouse's dreams of being a race car driver come true when she and her best friend Wilson enter a soap box derby.
ISBN 978-0-375-85713-3 (trade pbk.) — ISBN 978-0-375-95713-0 (lib. bdg.) —
ISBN 978-0-307-97940-7 (ebook)
1. Graphic novels. [1. Graphic novels. 2. Imagination—Fiction. 3. Soap box derbies—Fiction.
4. Mice—Fiction. 5. Animals—Fiction. 6. Humorous stories.]
I. Holm, Matthew. II. Title. III. Title: Burns rubber.
PZ7.7.H65Bad 2010 741.5'973—dc22 2009018819

MANUFACTURED IN MALAYSIA 20 19 18 17 16 15 14 13 12 11 10 9 8 7 First Edition

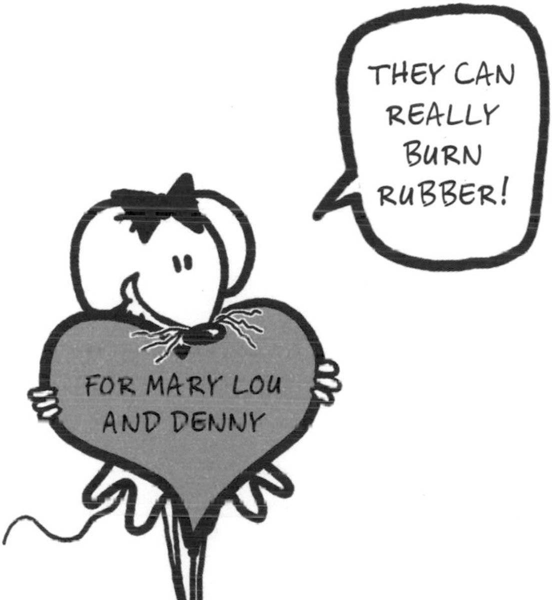
THEY CAN REALLY BURN RUBBER!
FOR MARY LOU AND DENNY

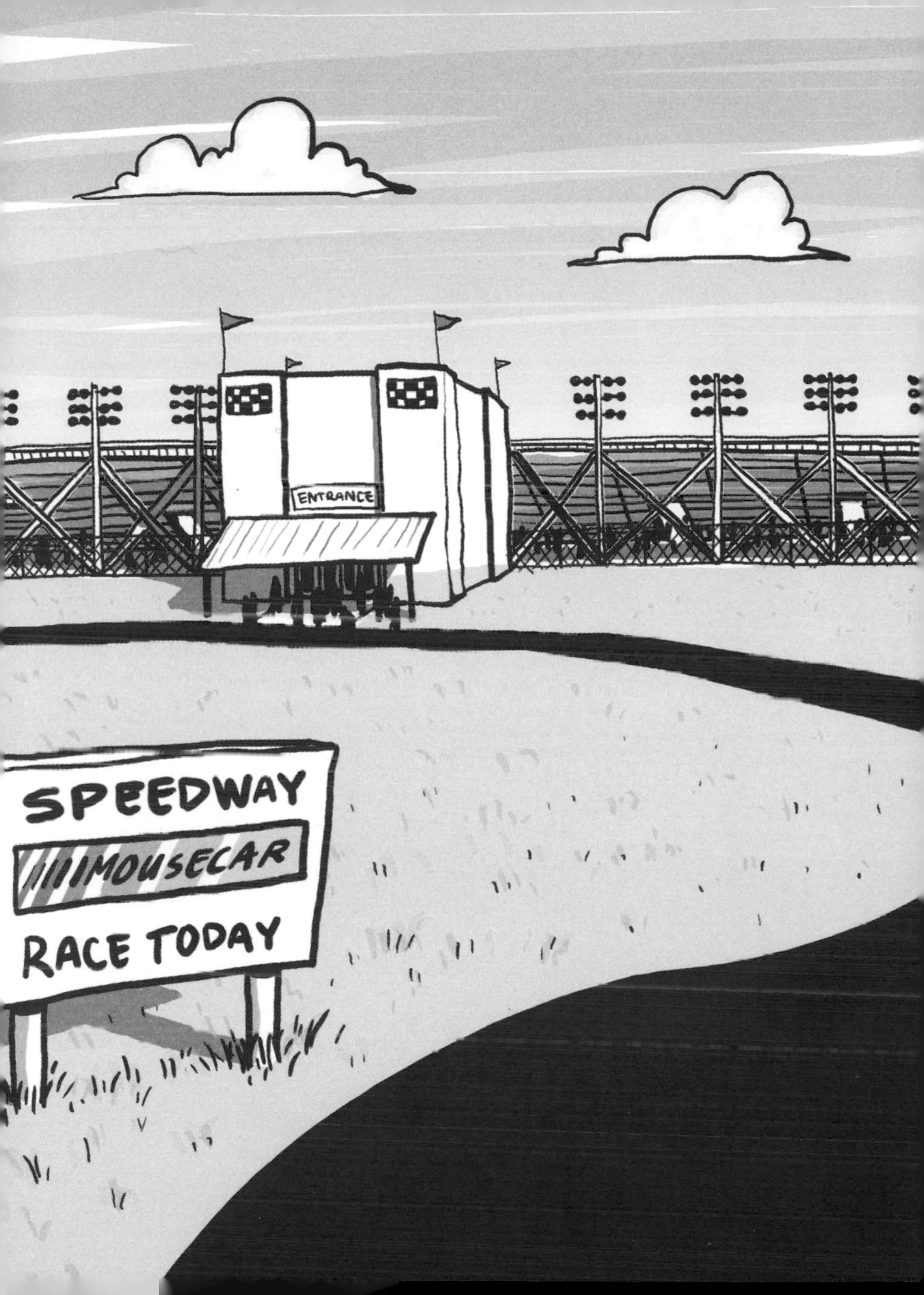
ENTRANCE
SPEEDWAY
MOUSECAR
RACE TODAY

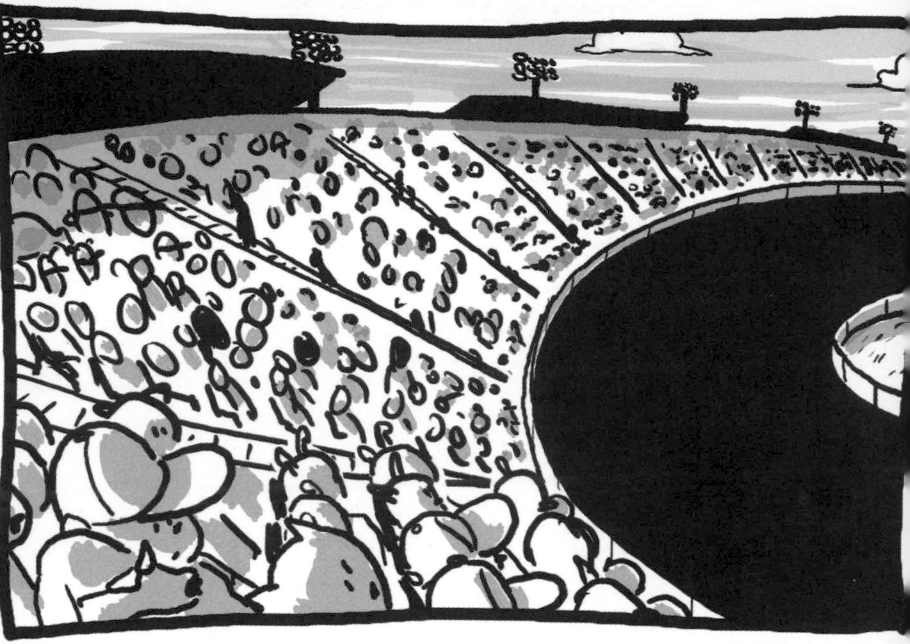

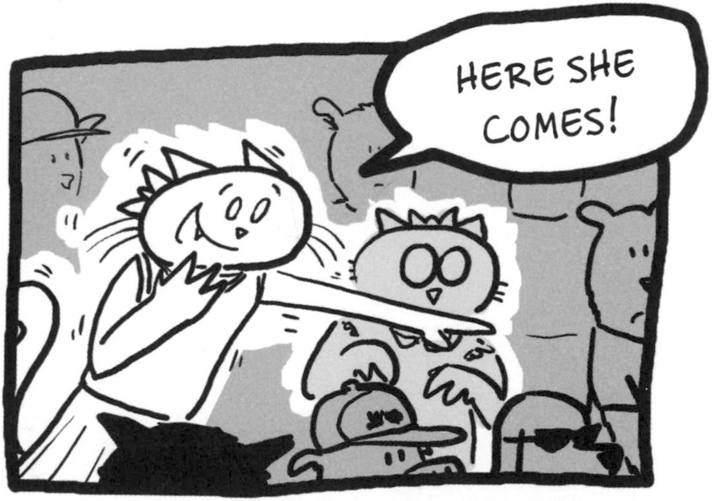
HERE SHE COMES!

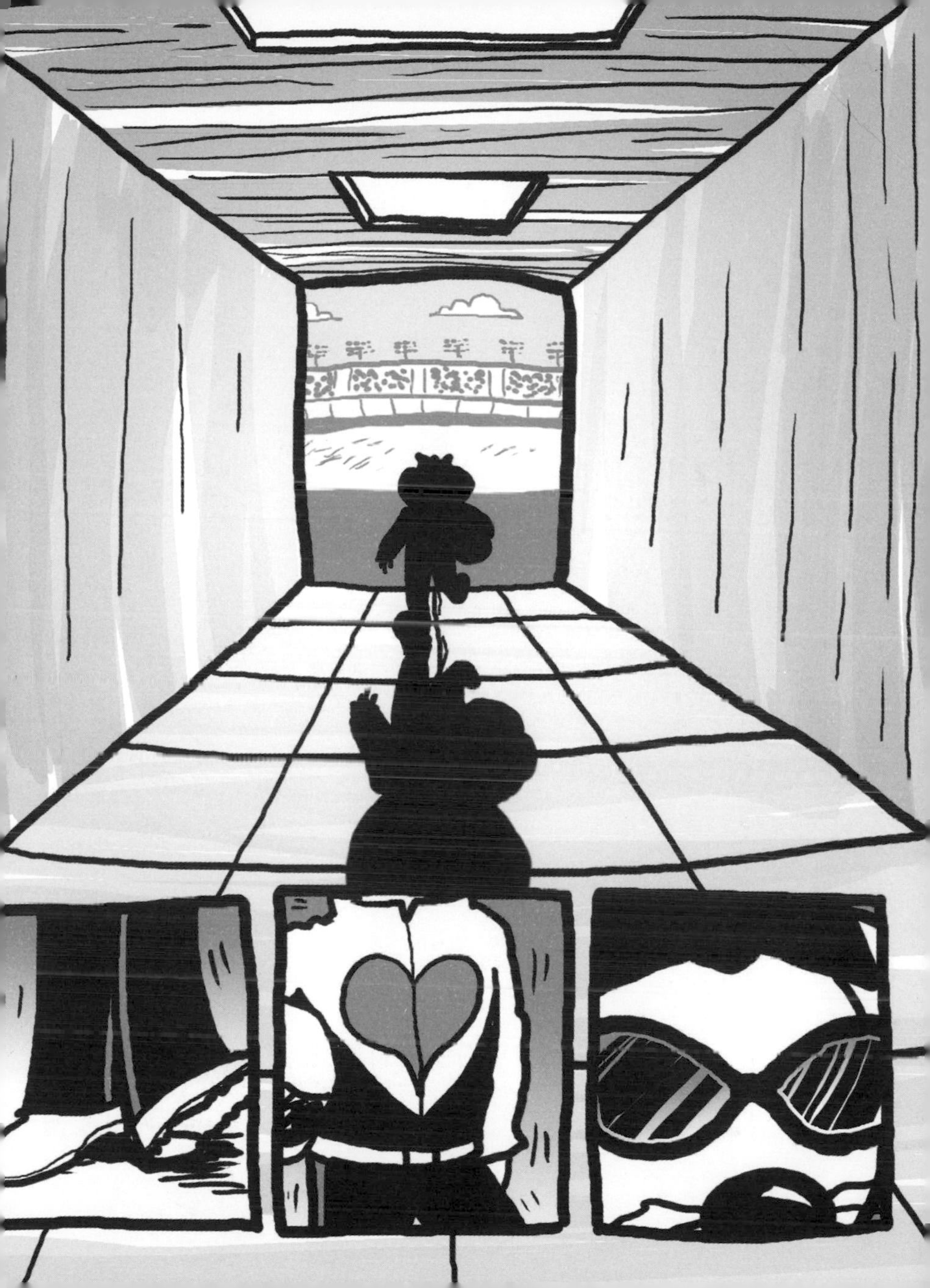

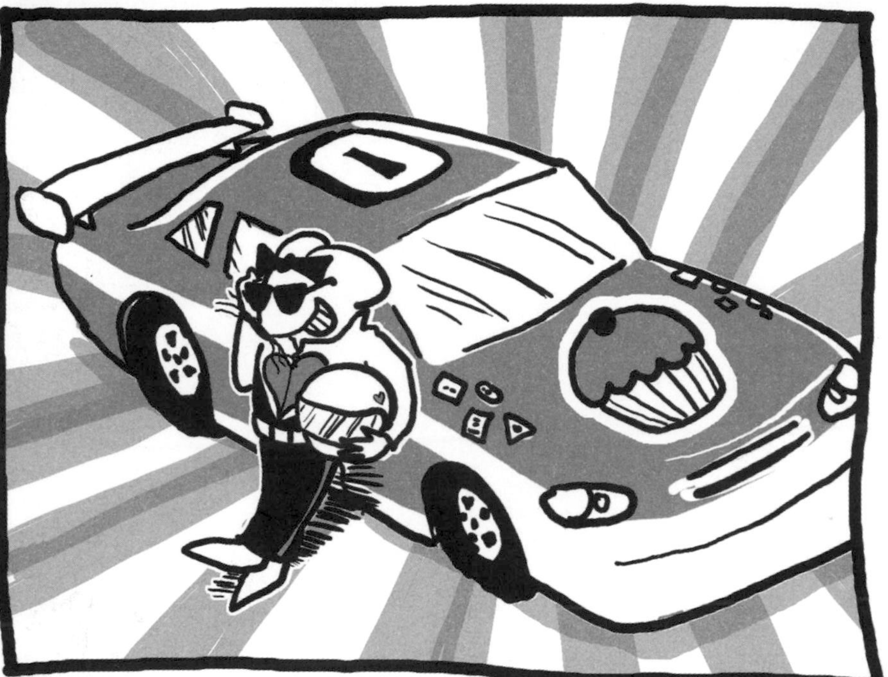

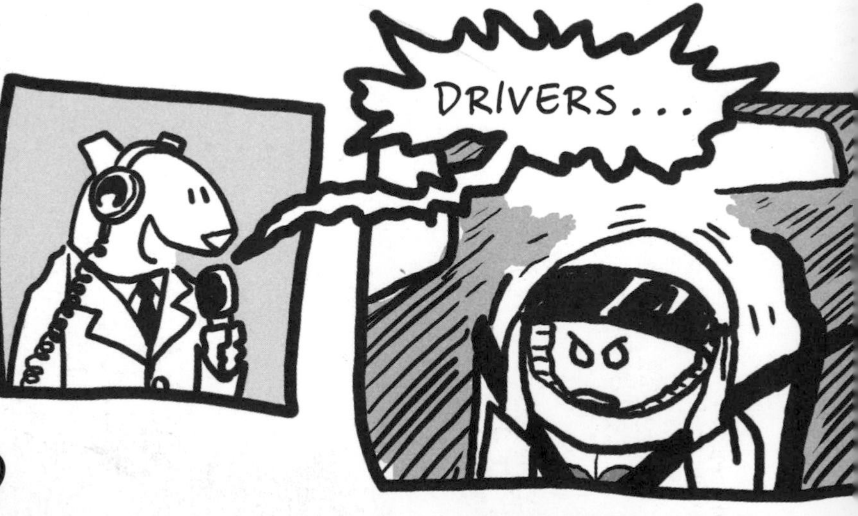
DRIVERS . . .

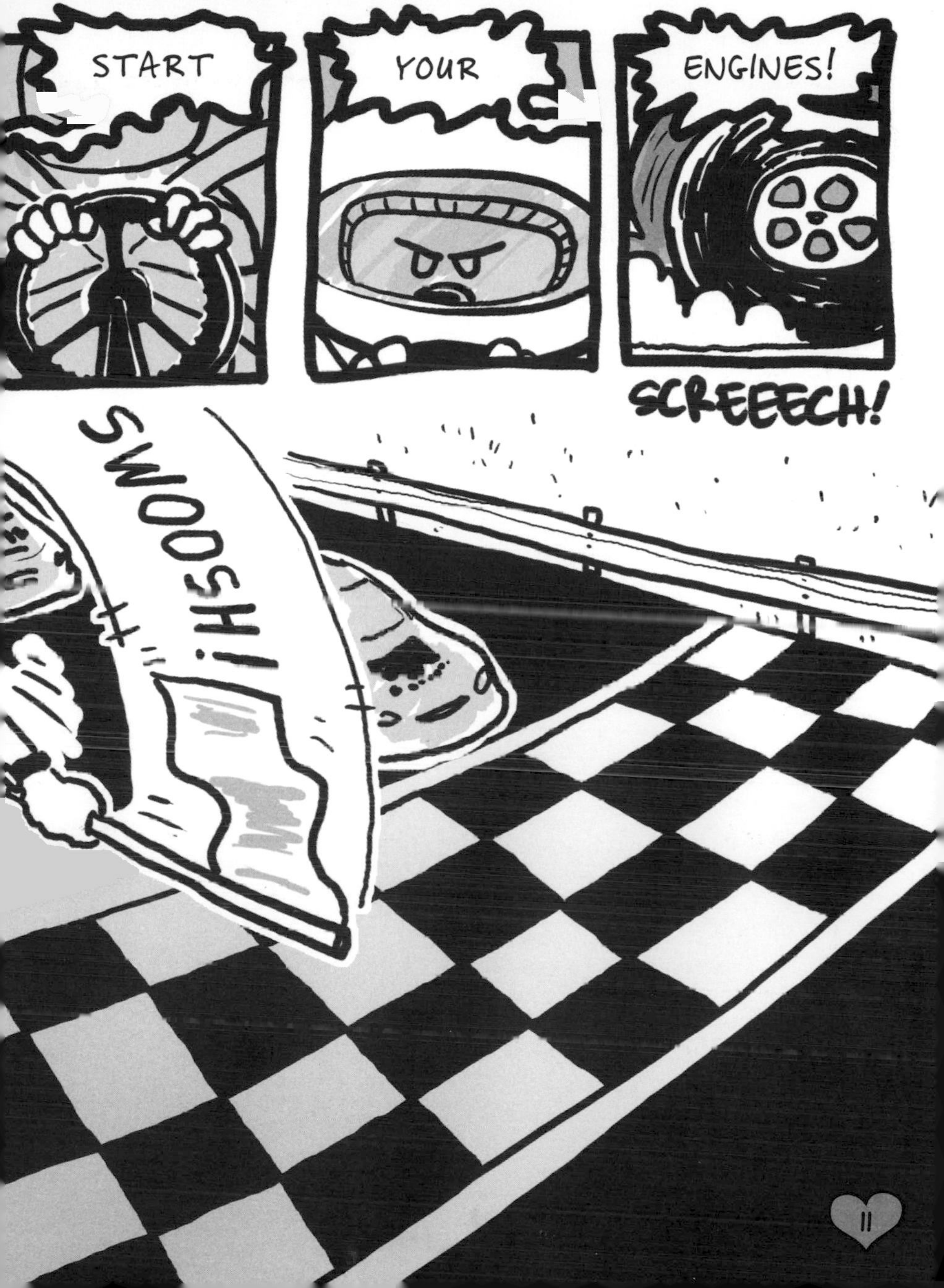
START
YOUR
ENGINES!
SCREEECH!
SWOOSH!

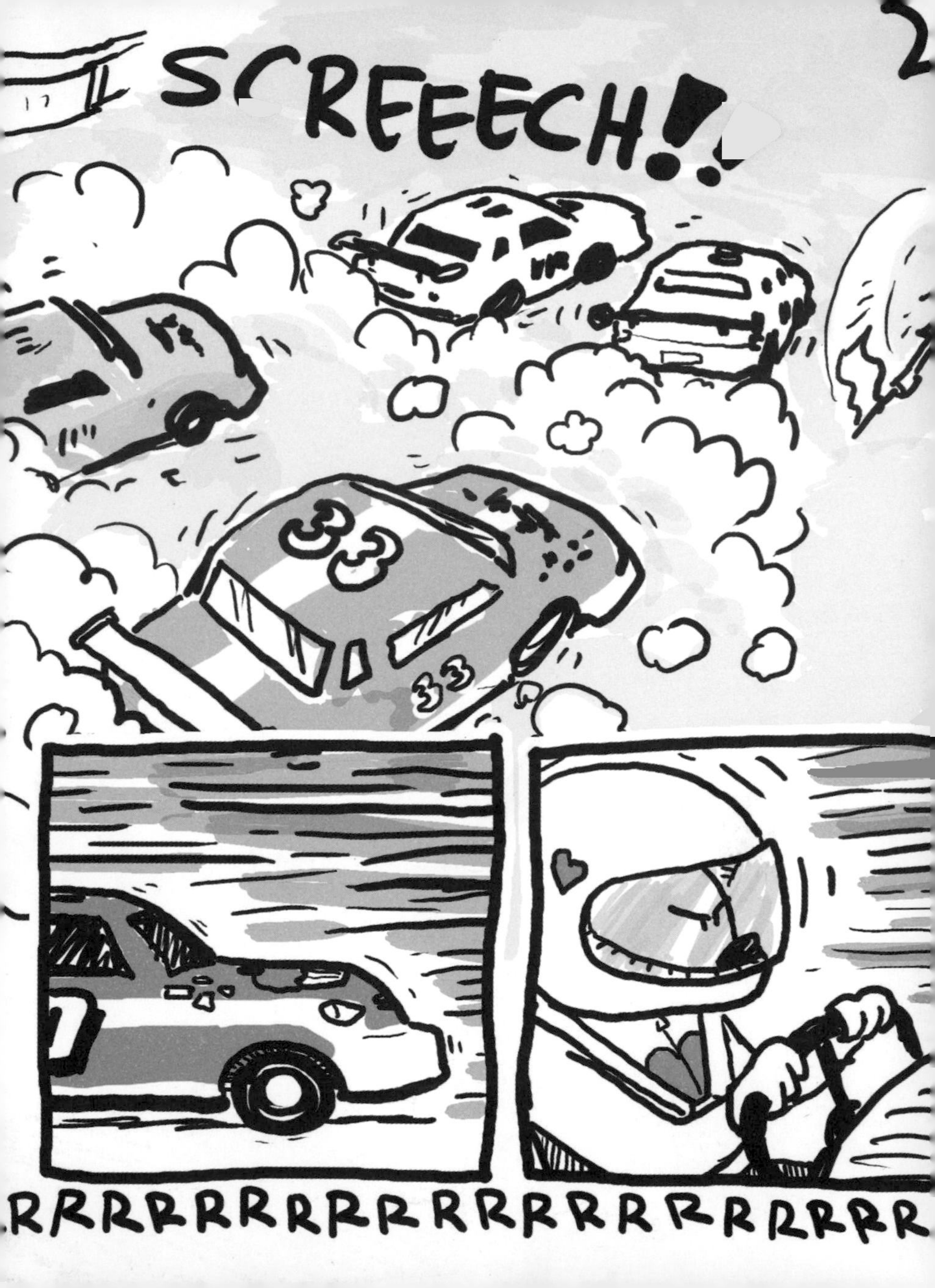
SCREEECH!!
RRRRRRRRRRRRRRRRRRR

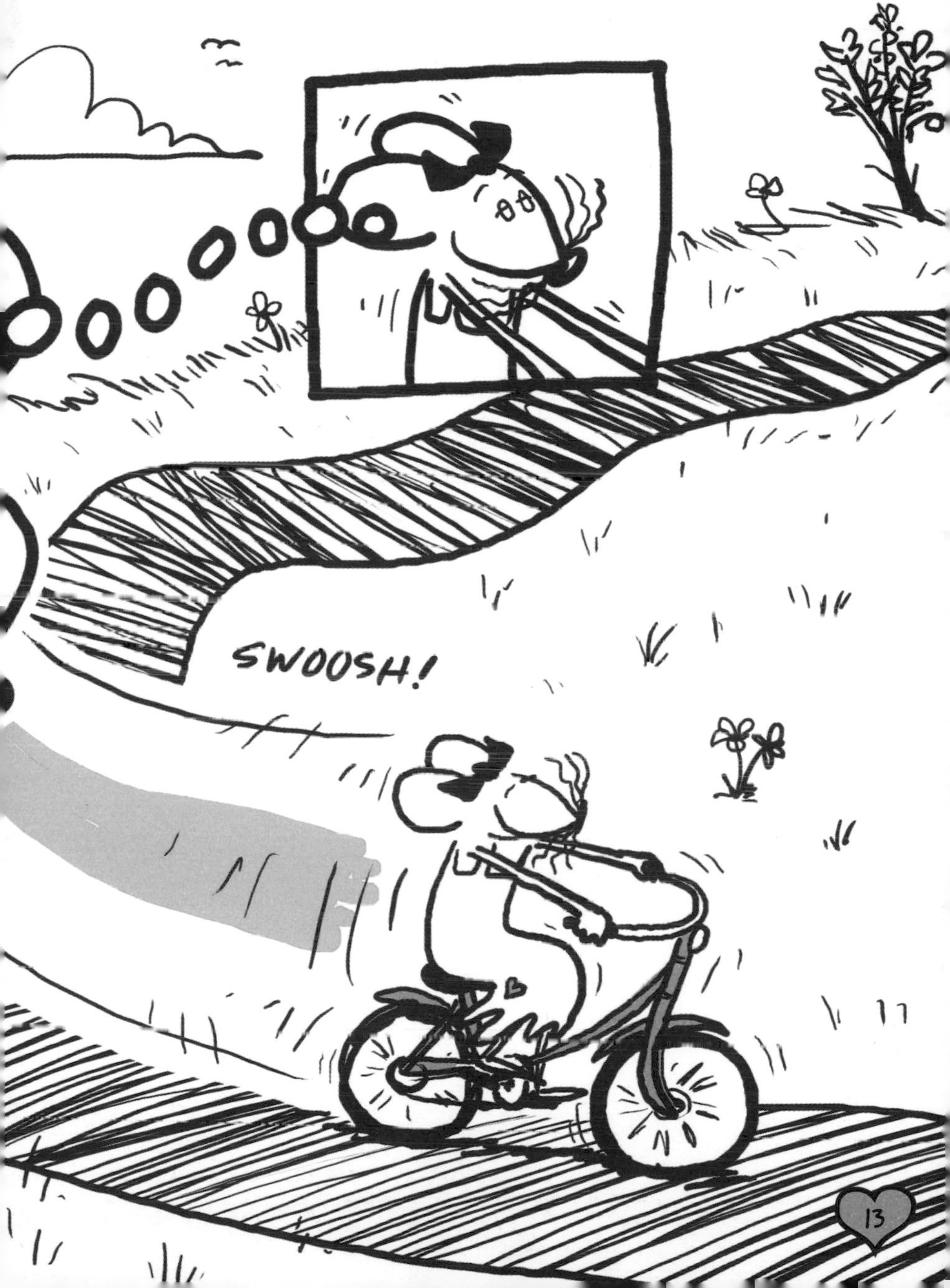
SWOOSH!

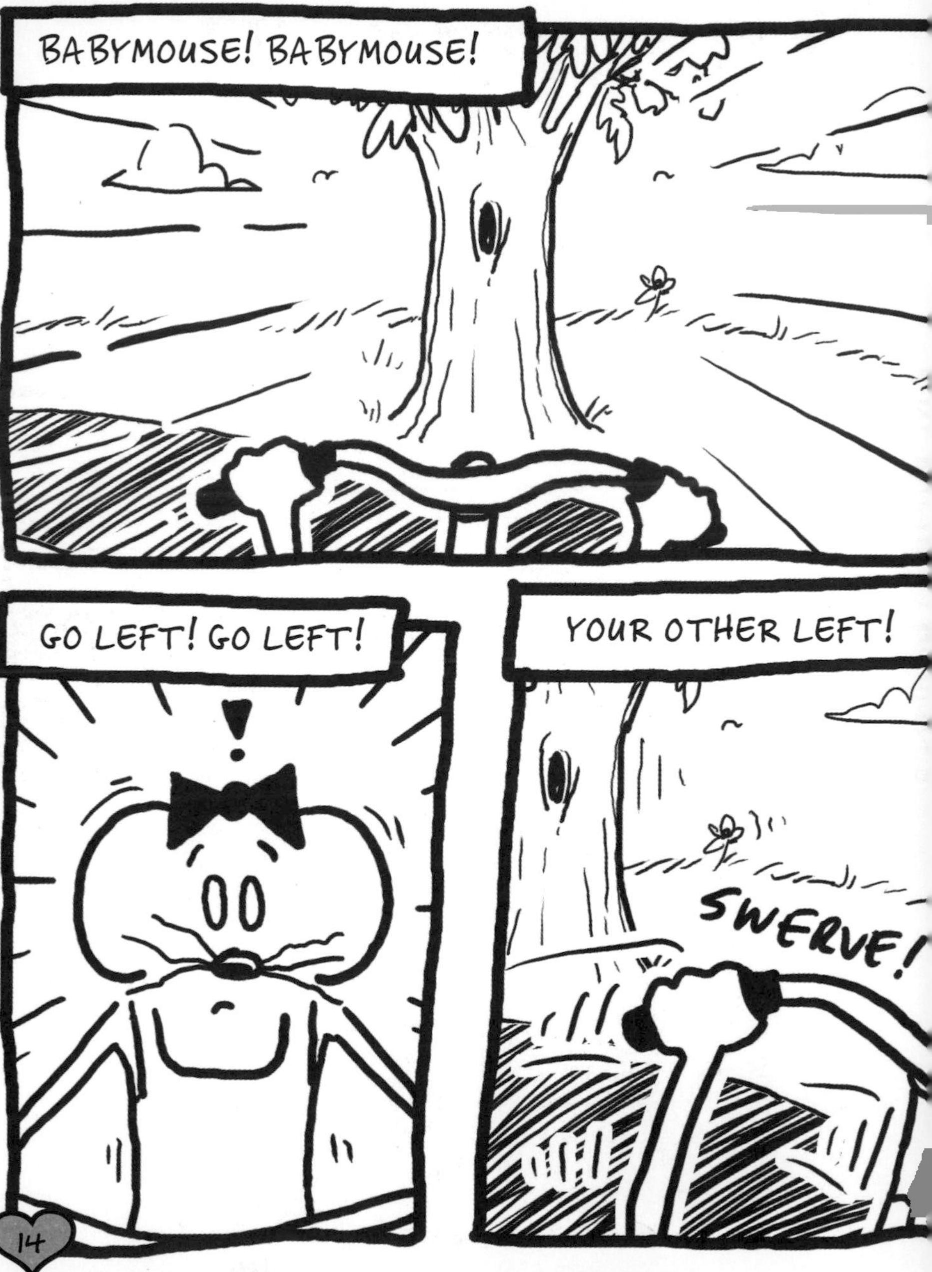

BABYMOUSE! BABYMOUSE!
GO LEFT! GO LEFT!
!
YOUR OTHER LEFT!
SWERVE!

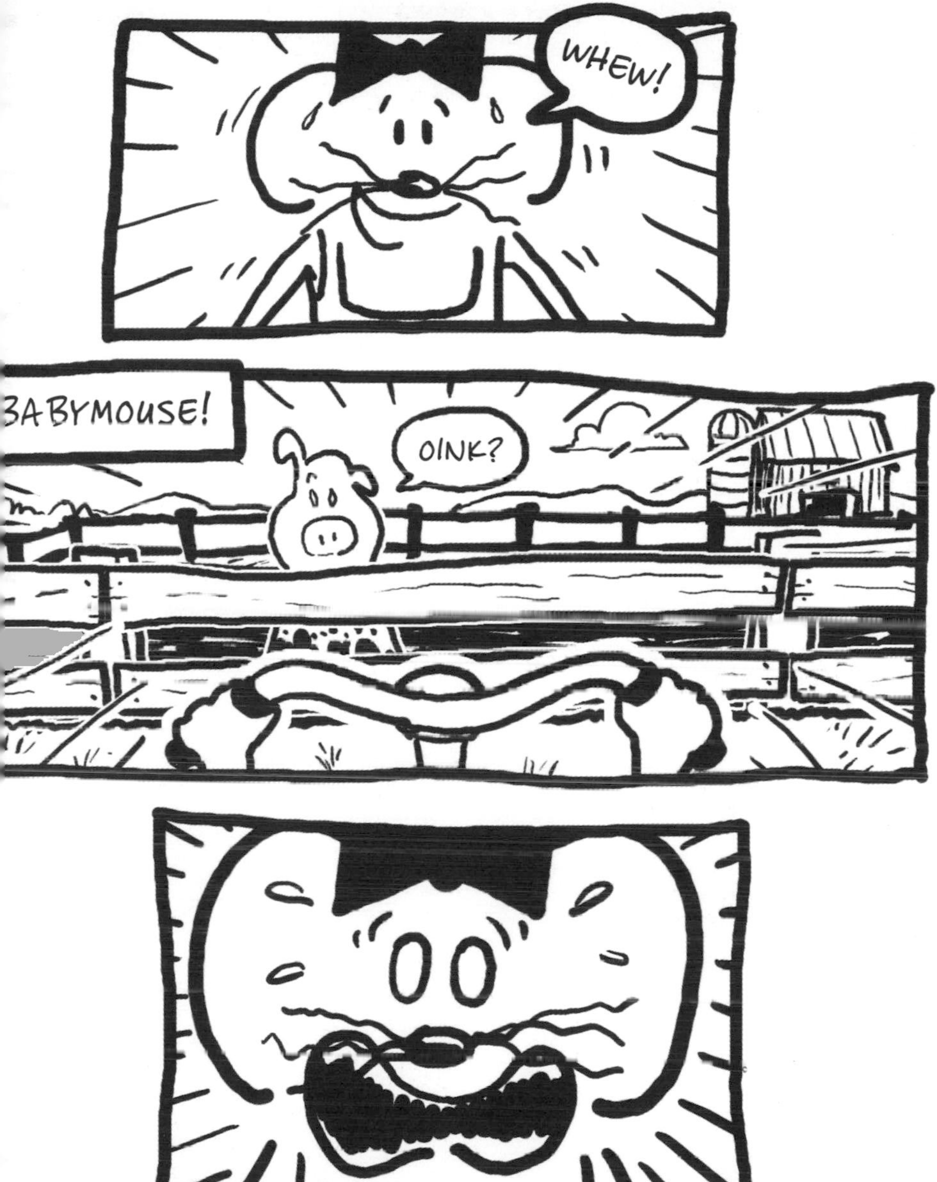
WHEW!
BABYMOUSE!
OINK?

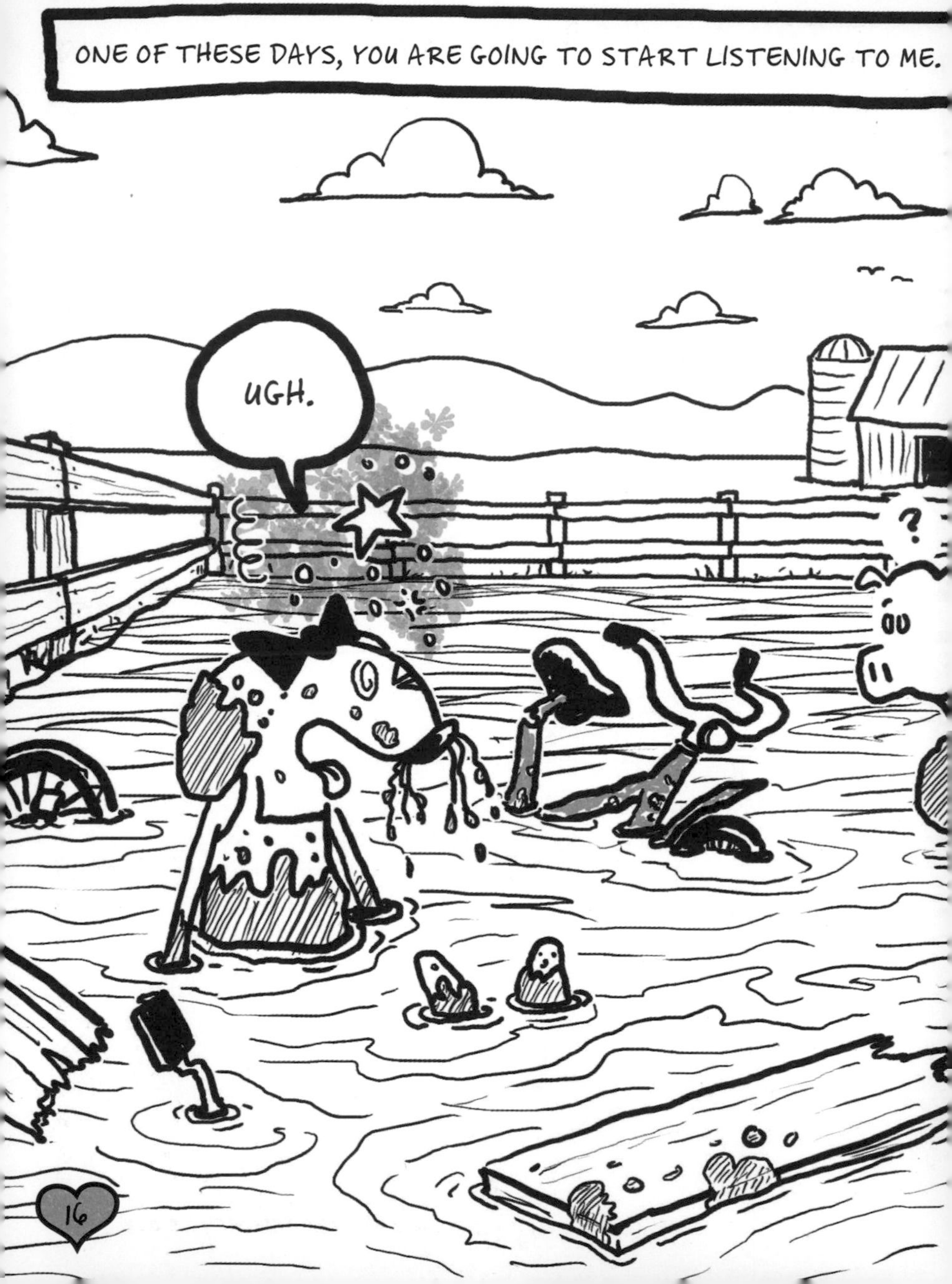
ONE OF THESE DAYS, YOU ARE GOING TO START LISTENING TO ME.
UGH.
?

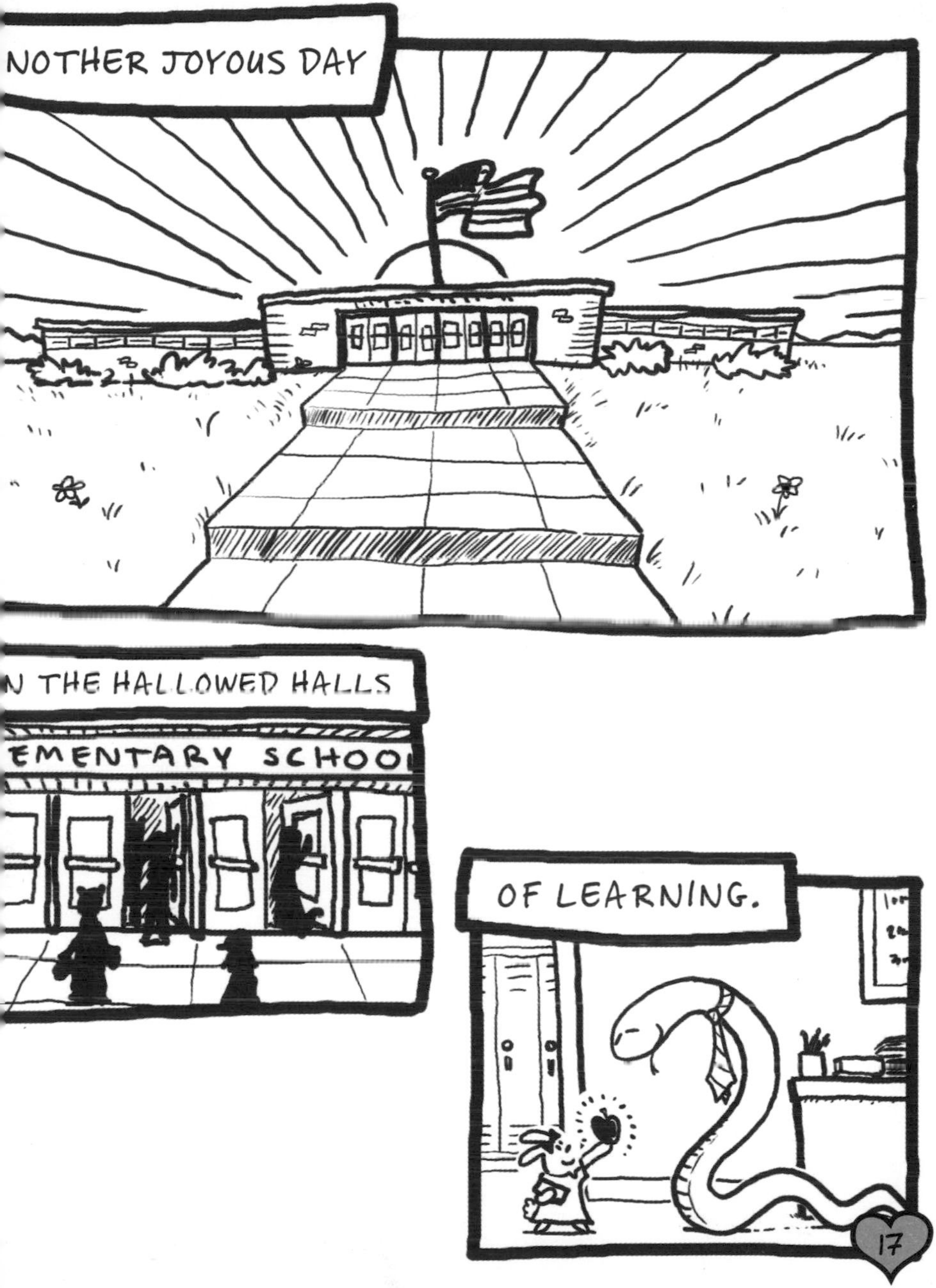
NOTHER JOYOUS DAY
N THE HALLOWED HALLS
EMENTARY SCHOO
OF LEARNING.

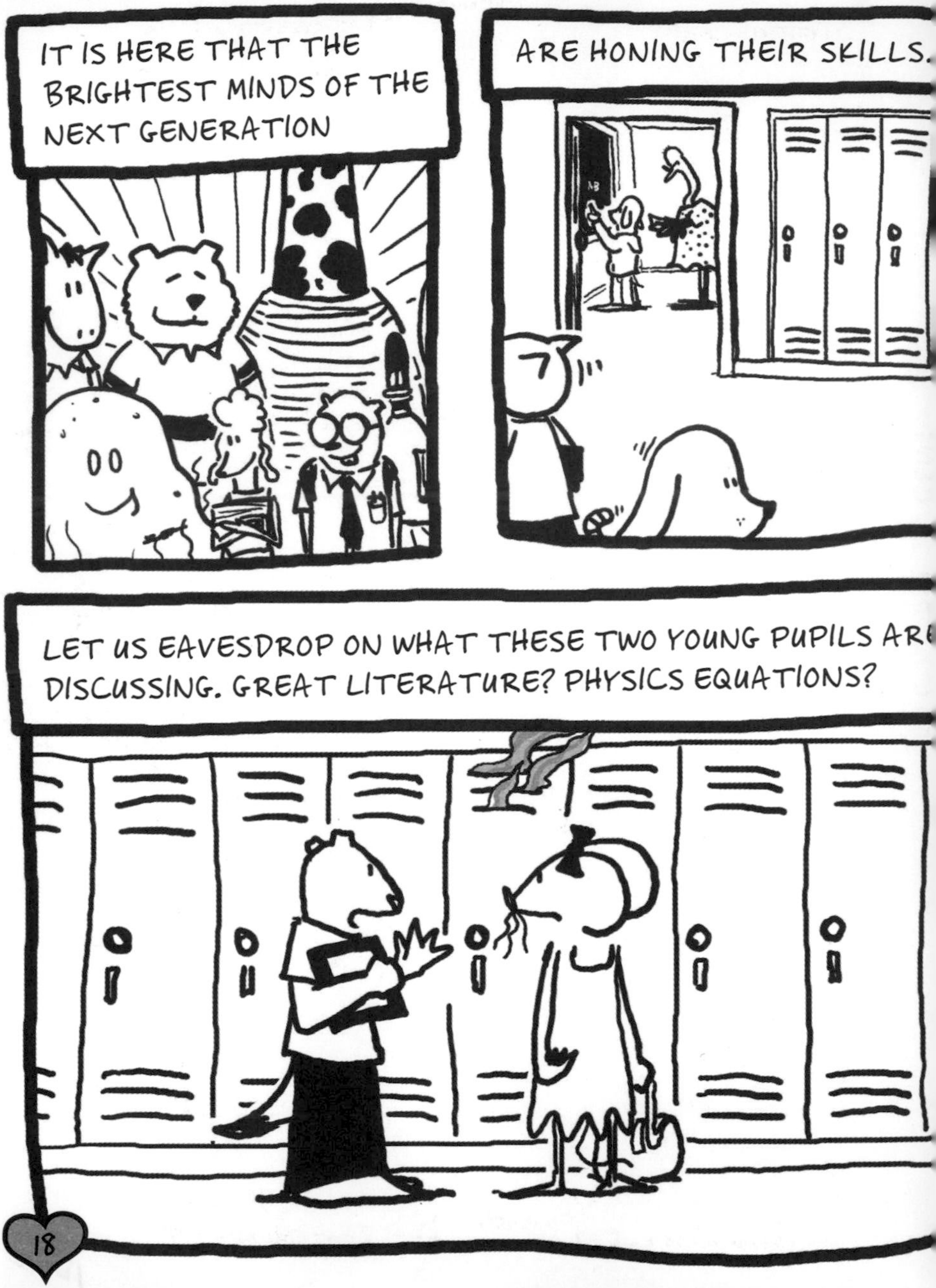
IT IS HERE THAT THE BRIGHTEST MINDS OF THE NEXT GENERATION
ARE HONING THEIR SKILLS.
LET US EAVESDROP ON WHAT THESE TWO YOUNG PUPILS ARE DISCUSSING. GREAT LITERATURE? PHYSICS EQUATIONS?

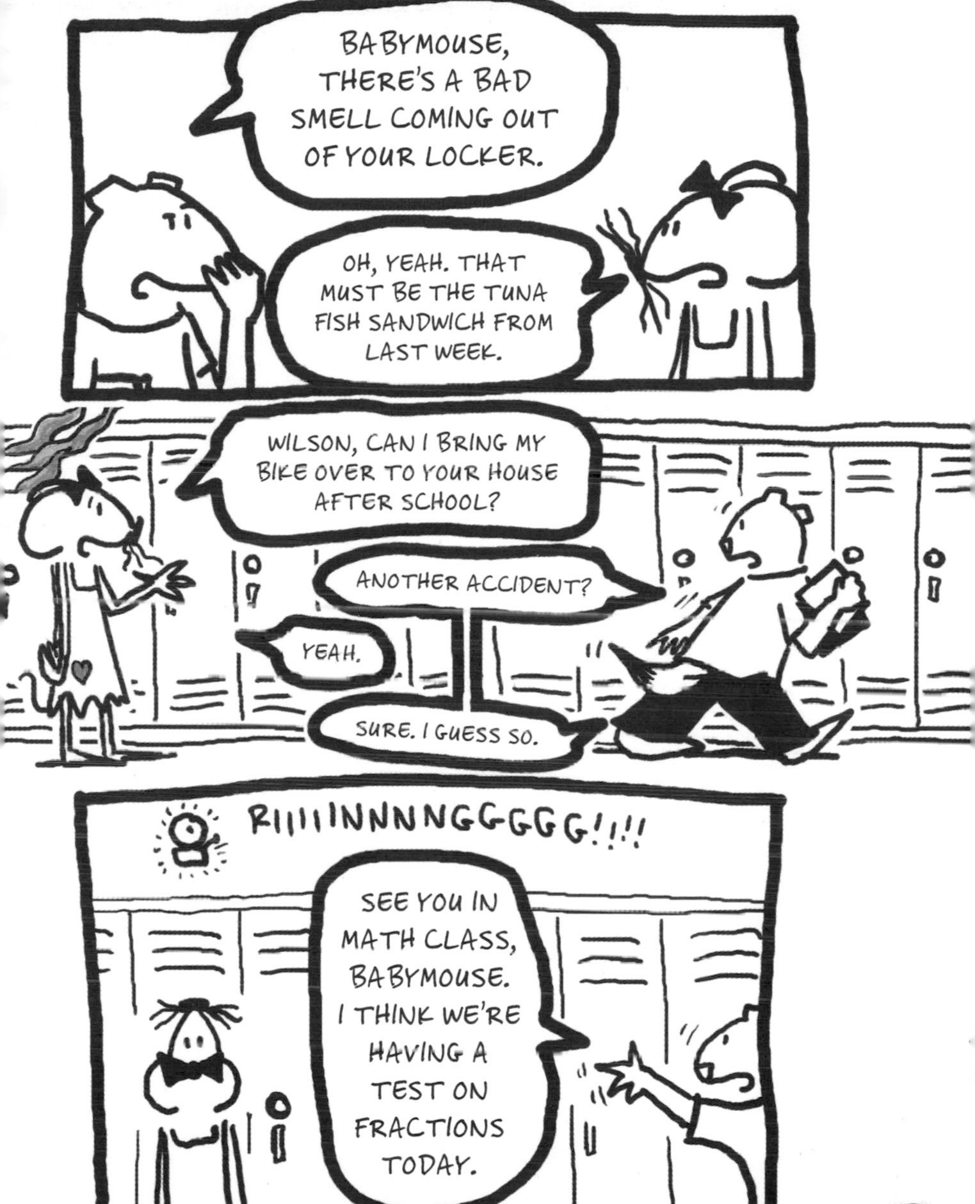

BABYMOUSE, THERE'S A BAD SMELL COMING OUT OF YOUR LOCKER.
OH, YEAH. THAT MUST BE THE TUNA FISH SANDWICH FROM LAST WEEK.
WILSON, CAN I BRING MY BIKE OVER TO YOUR HOUSE AFTER SCHOOL?
ANOTHER ACCIDENT?
YEAH.
SURE. I GUESS SO.
RIIIIINNNNGGGGG!!!!
SEE YOU IN MATH CLASS, BABYMOUSE. I THINK WE'RE HAVING A TEST ON FRACTIONS TODAY.

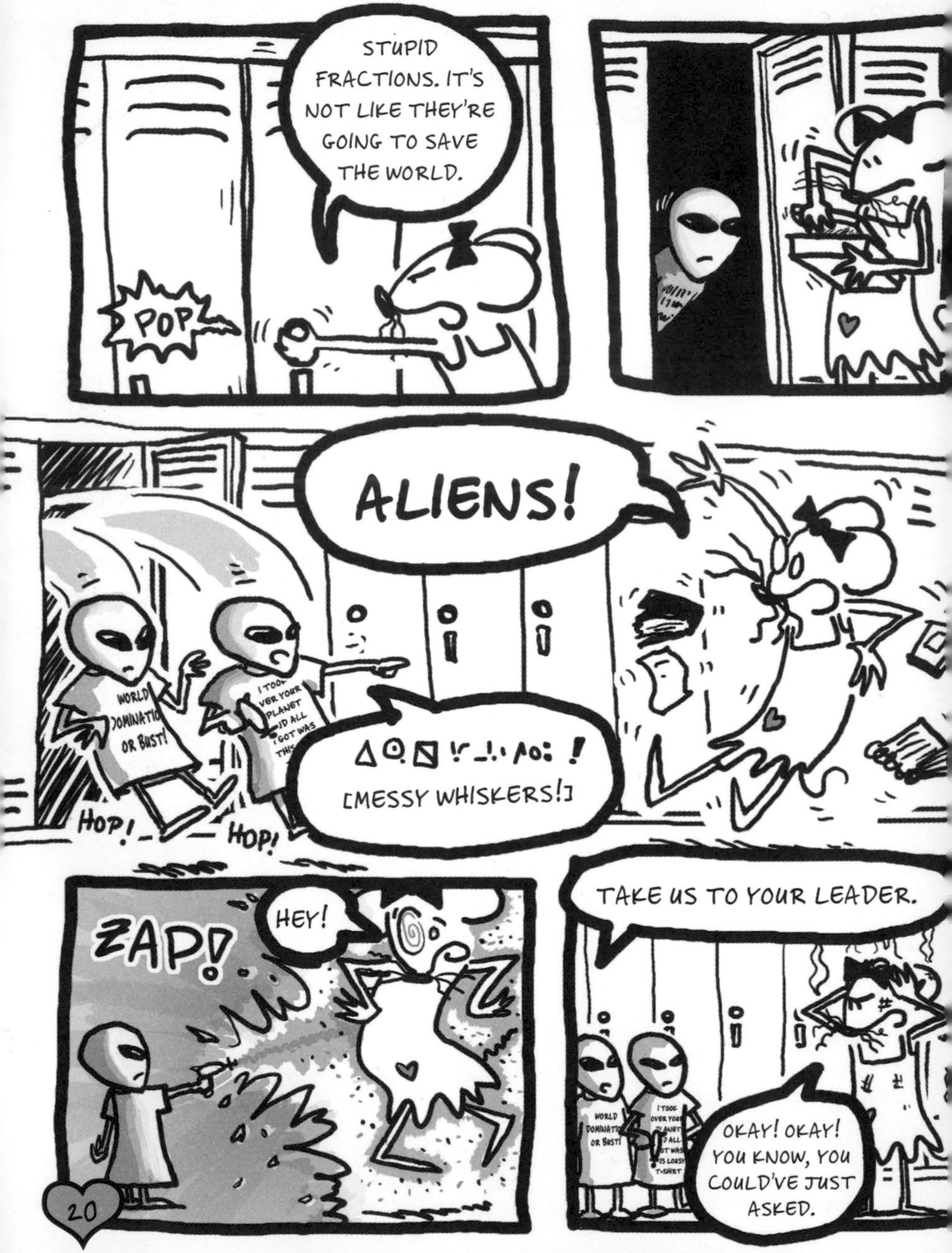

STUPID FRACTIONS. IT'S NOT LIKE THEY'RE GOING TO SAVE THE WORLD.
POP
ALIENS!
WORLD DOMINATIO OR BUST!
[MESSY WHISKERS!]
HOP! HOP!
ZAP!
HEY!
TAKE US TO YOUR LEADER.
OKAY! OKAY! YOU KNOW, YOU COULD'VE JUST ASKED.

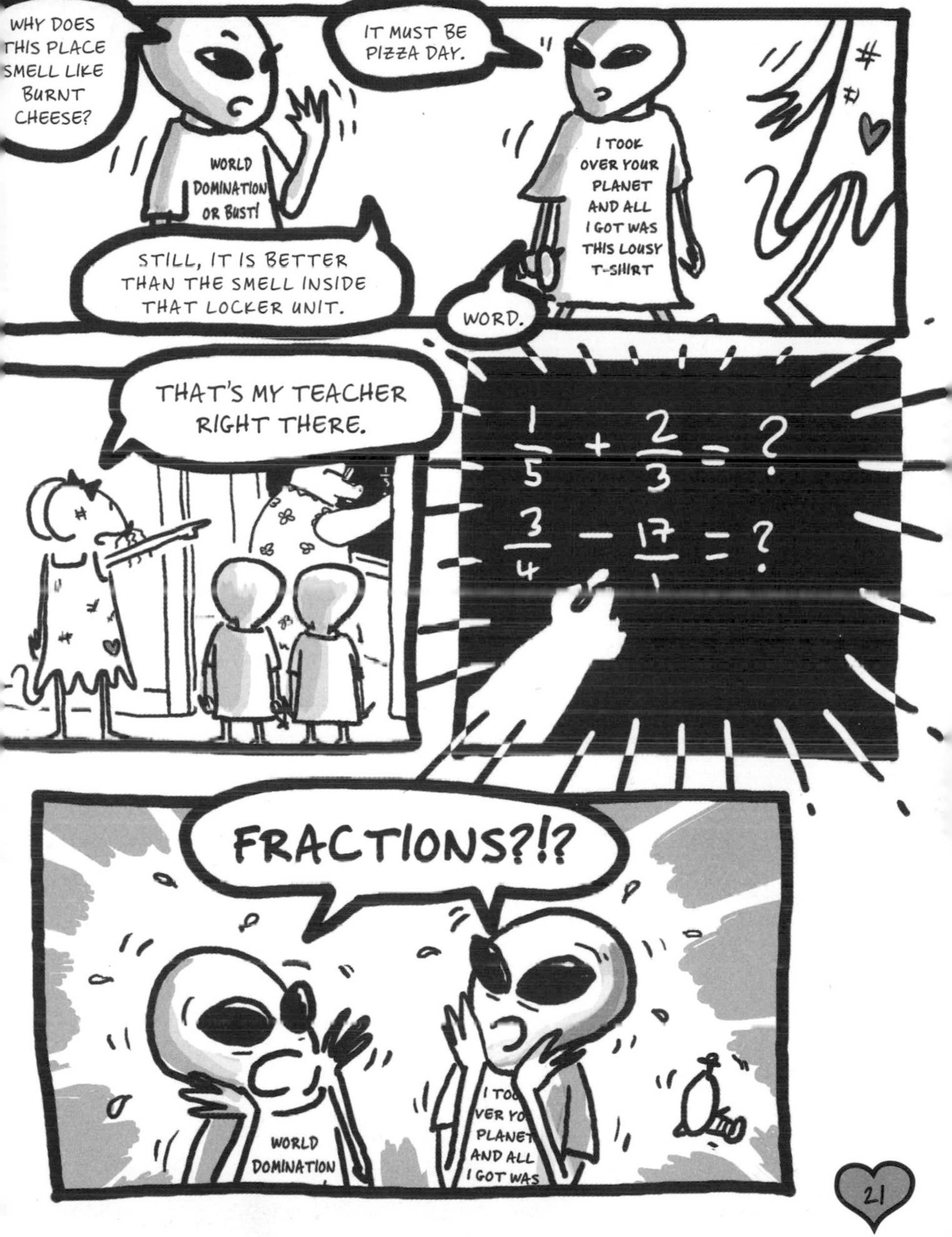
WHY DOES THIS PLACE SMELL LIKE BURNT CHEESE?
WORLD DOMINATION OR BUST!
IT MUST BE PIZZA DAY.
I TOOK OVER YOUR PLANET AND ALL I GOT WAS THIS LOUSY T-SHIRT
STILL, IT IS BETTER THAN THE SMELL INSIDE THAT LOCKER UNIT.
WORD.
THAT'S MY TEACHER RIGHT THERE.
1/5 + 2/3 = ?
3/4 − 17/1 = ?
FRACTIONS?!?
WORLD DOMINATION
I TOO VER YO PLANET AND ALL I GOT WAS

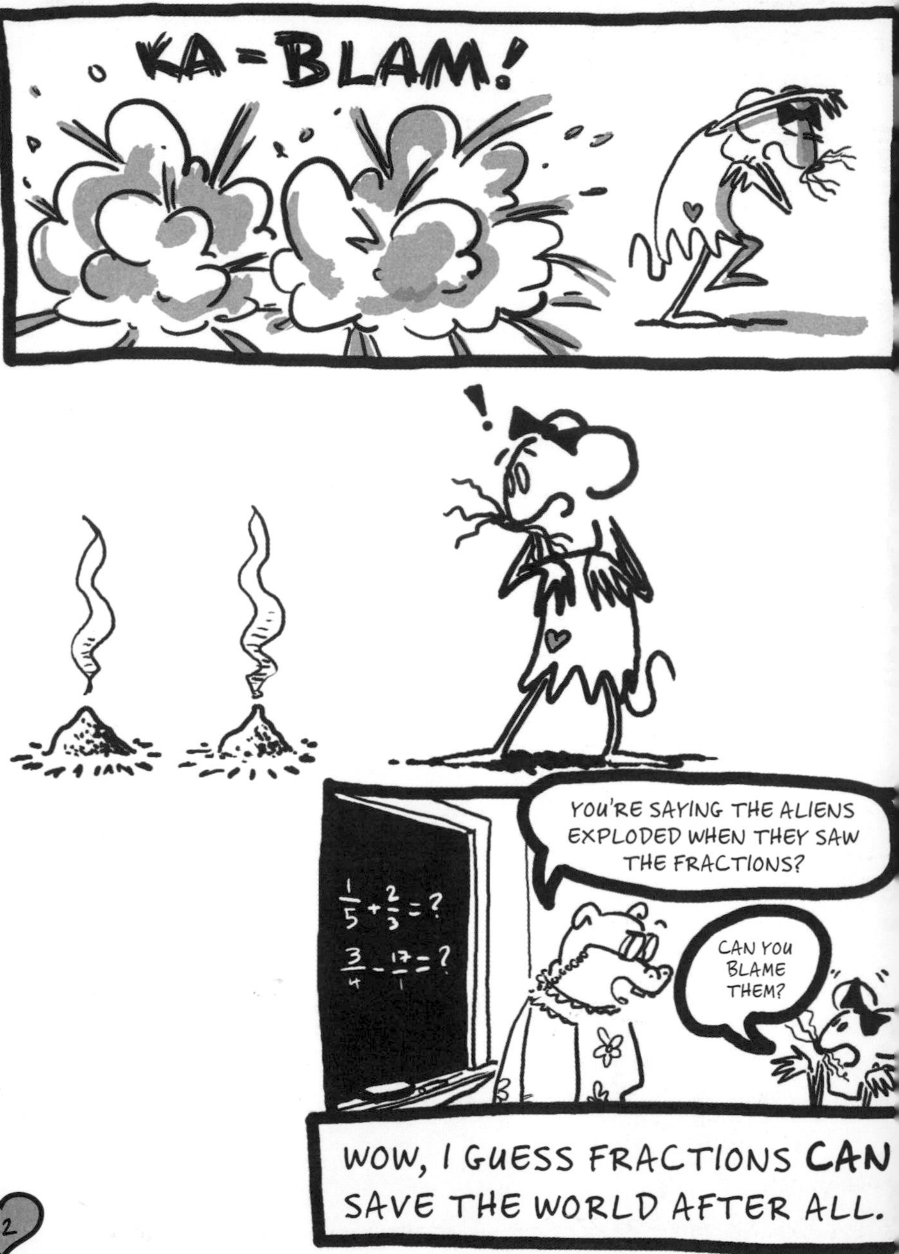
KA-BLAM!
!
YOU'RE SAYING THE ALIENS EXPLODED WHEN THEY SAW THE FRACTIONS?
$\frac{1}{5}+\frac{2}{3}=?$
$\frac{3}{4}-\frac{17}{1}=?$
CAN YOU BLAME THEM?
WOW, I GUESS FRACTIONS **CAN** SAVE THE WORLD AFTER ALL.

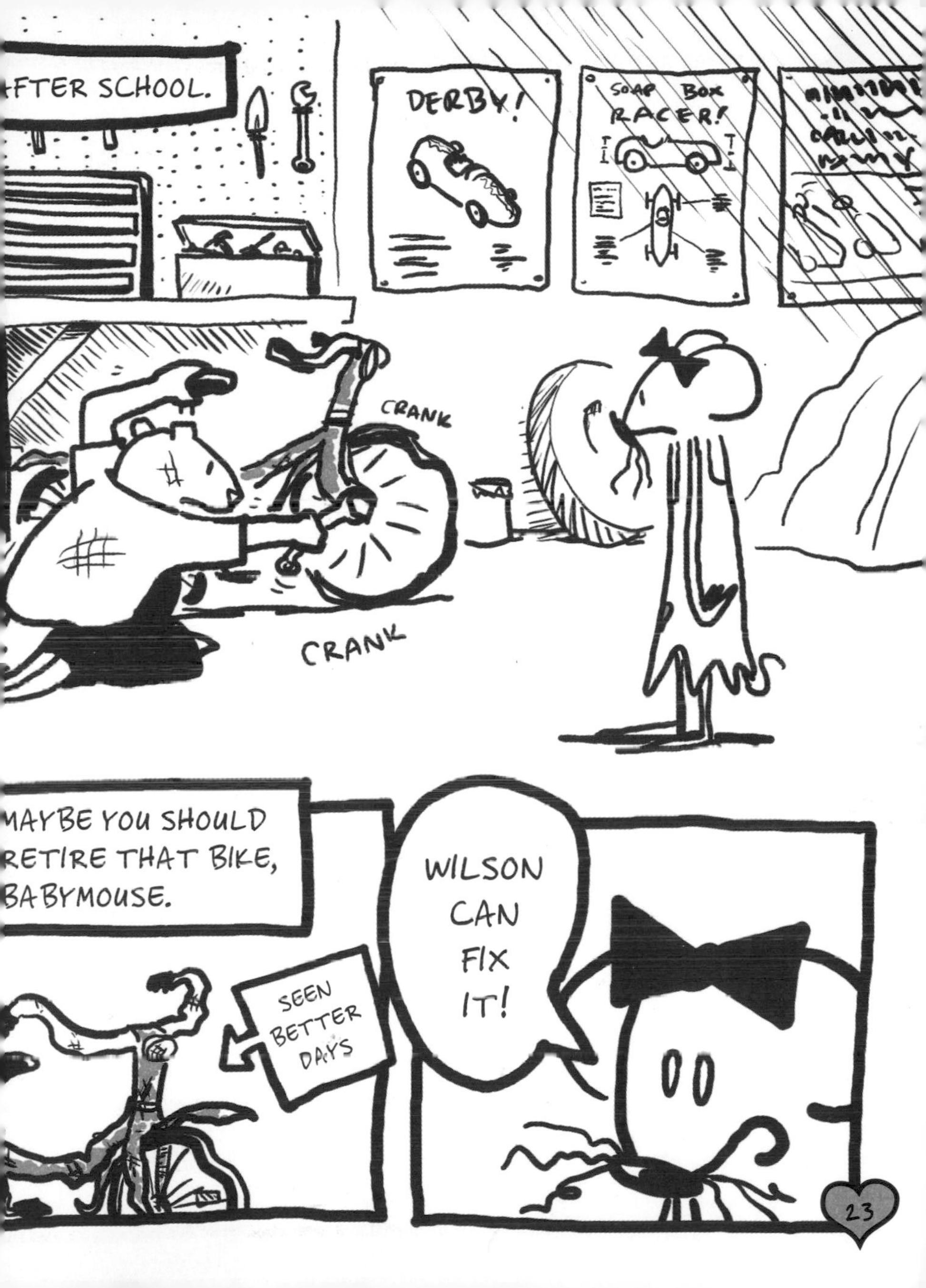
AFTER SCHOOL.
DERBY!
SOAP BOX RACER!
CRANK
CRANK
MAYBE YOU SHOULD RETIRE THAT BIKE, BABYMOUSE.
SEEN BETTER DAYS
WILSON CAN FIX IT!

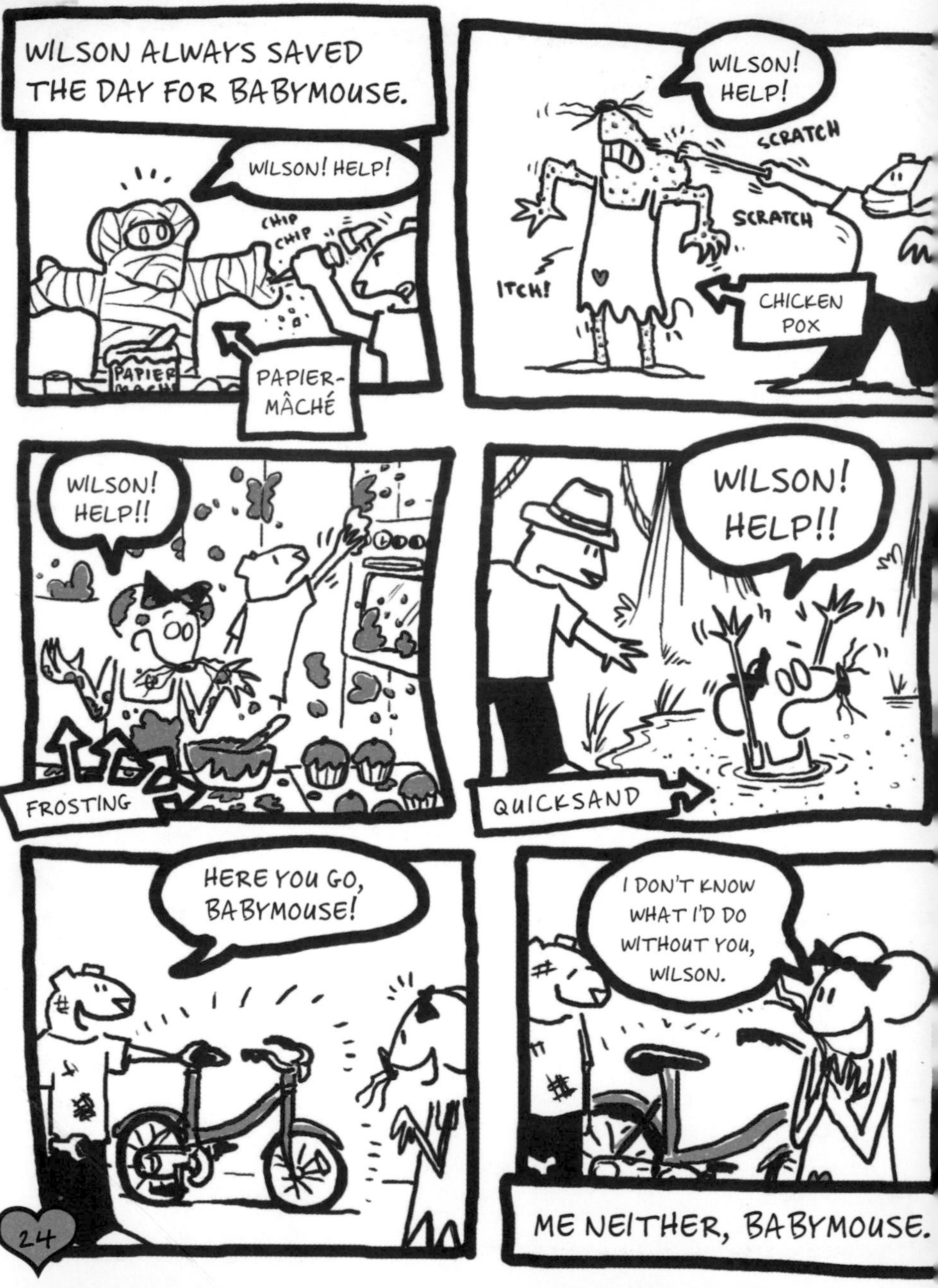

WILSON ALWAYS SAVED THE DAY FOR BABYMOUSE.
WILSON! HELP!
CHIP CHIP
PAPIER MACHE
PAPIER-MÂCHÉ
WILSON! HELP!
SCRATCH
SCRATCH
ITCH!
CHICKEN POX
WILSON! HELP!!
FROSTING
WILSON! HELP!!
QUICKSAND
HERE YOU GO, BABYMOUSE!
I DON'T KNOW WHAT I'D DO WITHOUT YOU, WILSON.
ME NEITHER, BABYMOUSE.

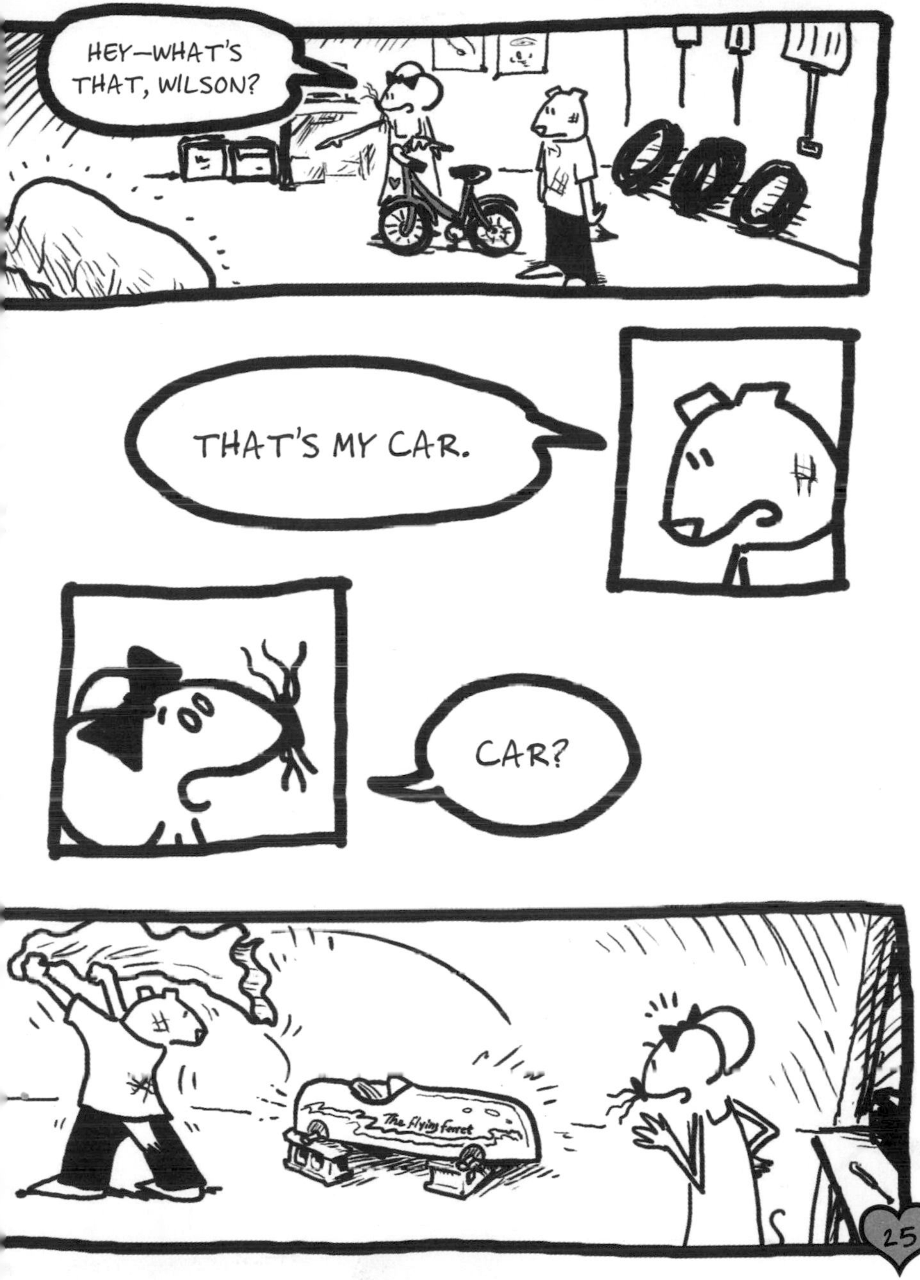
HEY—WHAT'S THAT, WILSON?
THAT'S MY CAR.
CAR?
The flying ferret

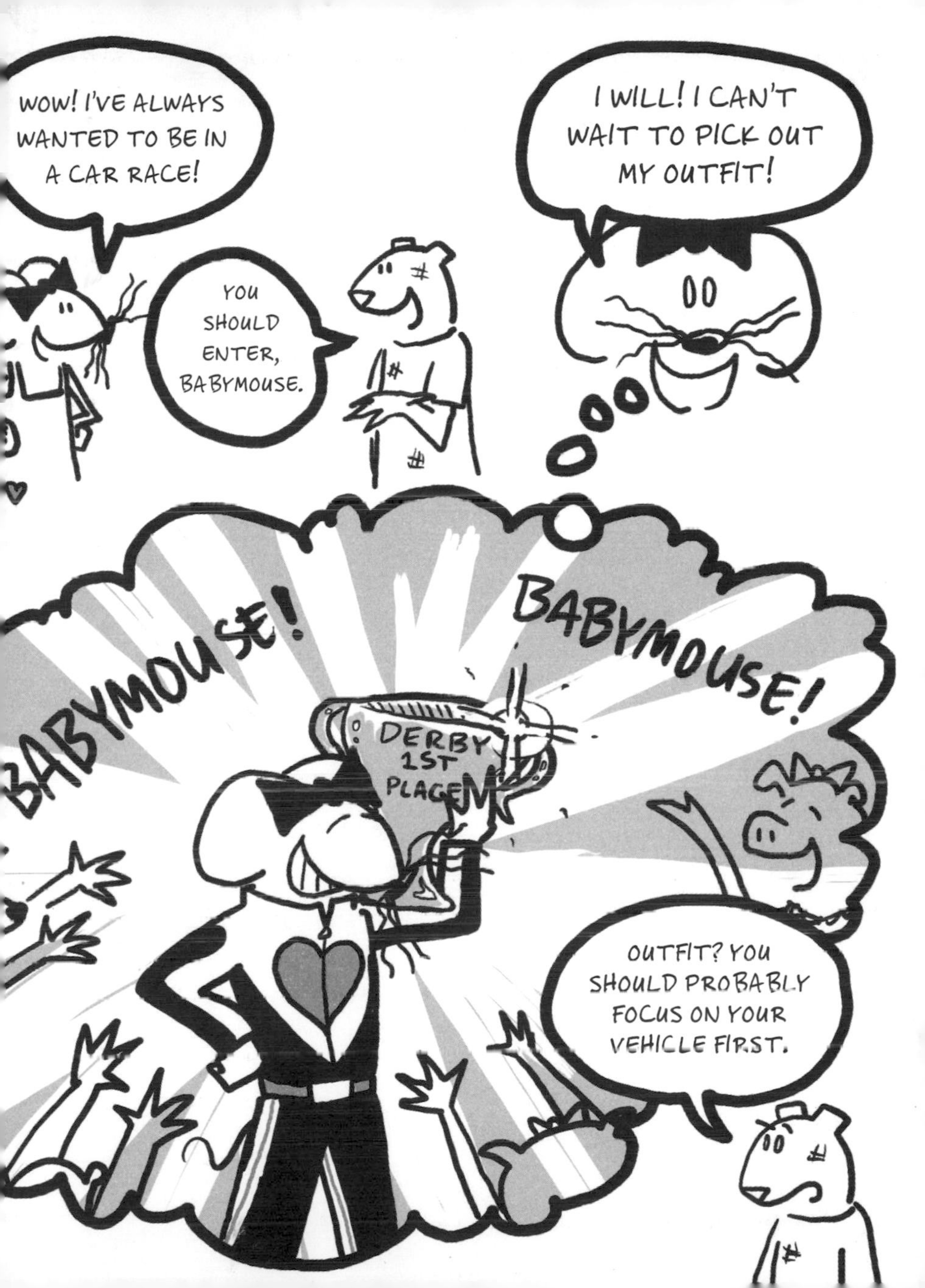
WOW! I'VE ALWAYS WANTED TO BE IN A CAR RACE!
YOU SHOULD ENTER, BABYMOUSE.
I WILL! I CAN'T WAIT TO PICK OUT MY OUTFIT!
BABYMOUSE!
BABYMOUSE!
DERBY 1ST PLACE
OUTFIT? YOU SHOULD PROBABLY FOCUS ON YOUR VEHICLE FIRST.

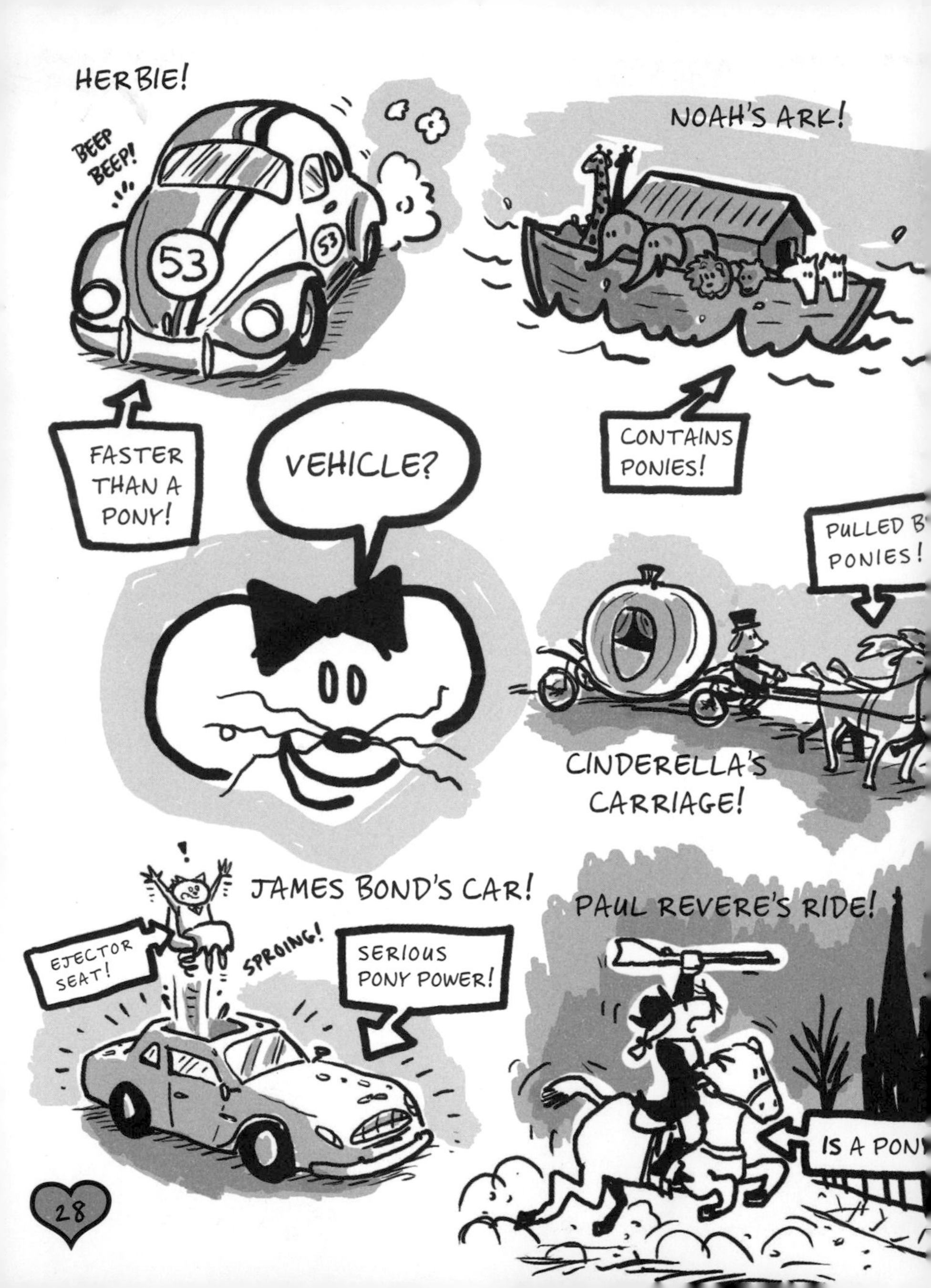
HERBIE!
BEEP BEEP!
53
FASTER THAN A PONY!
NOAH'S ARK!
CONTAINS PONIES!
VEHICLE?
PULLED BY PONIES!
CINDERELLA'S CARRIAGE!
JAMES BOND'S CAR!
EJECTOR SEAT!
SPROING!
SERIOUS PONY POWER!
PAUL REVERE'S RIDE!
IS A PONY

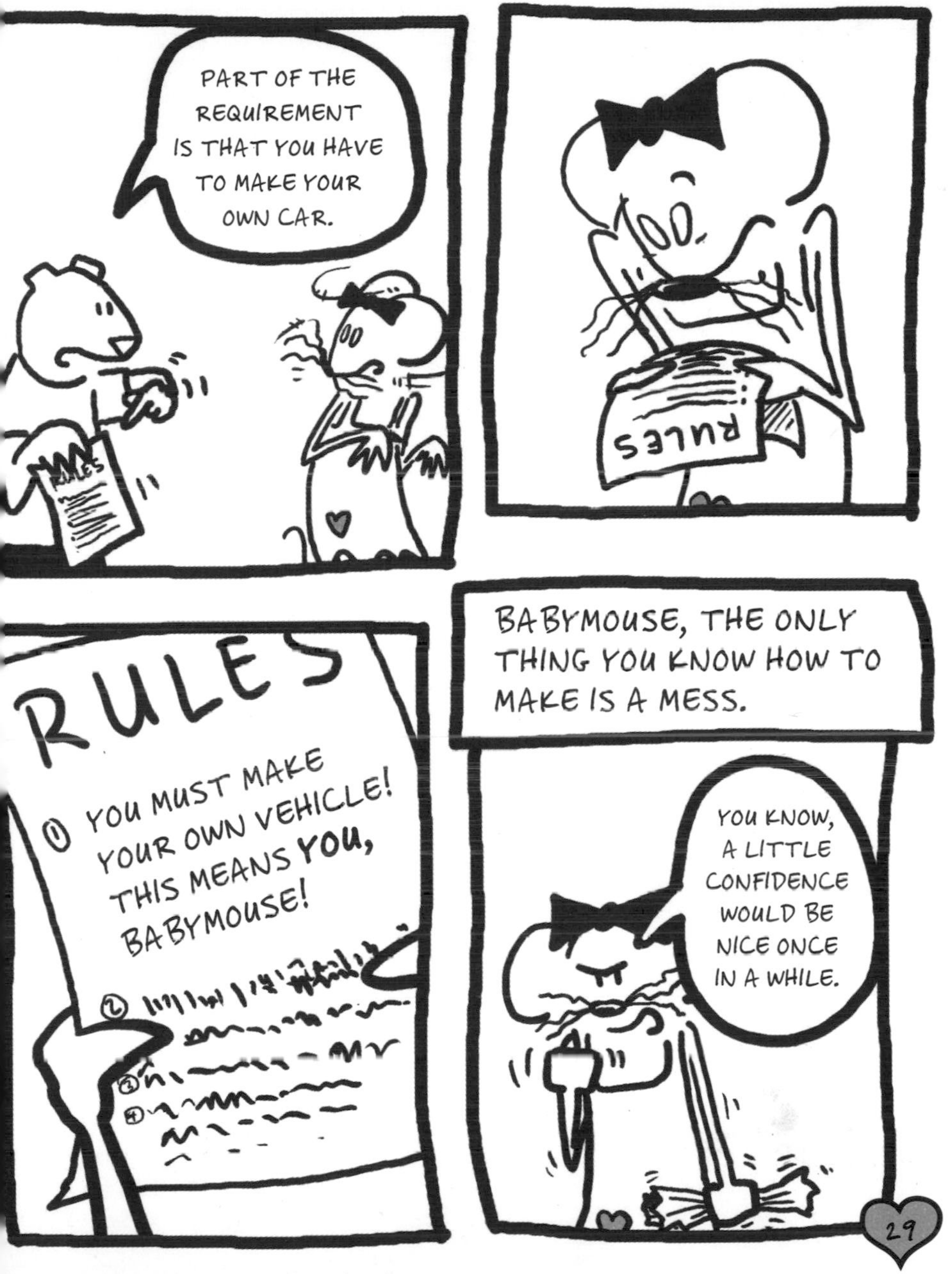
PART OF THE REQUIREMENT IS THAT YOU HAVE TO MAKE YOUR OWN CAR.
RULES
RULES
RULES
① YOU MUST MAKE YOUR OWN VEHICLE! THIS MEANS **YOU**, BABYMOUSE!
BABYMOUSE, THE ONLY THING YOU KNOW HOW TO MAKE IS A MESS.
YOU KNOW, A LITTLE CONFIDENCE WOULD BE NICE ONCE IN A WHILE.

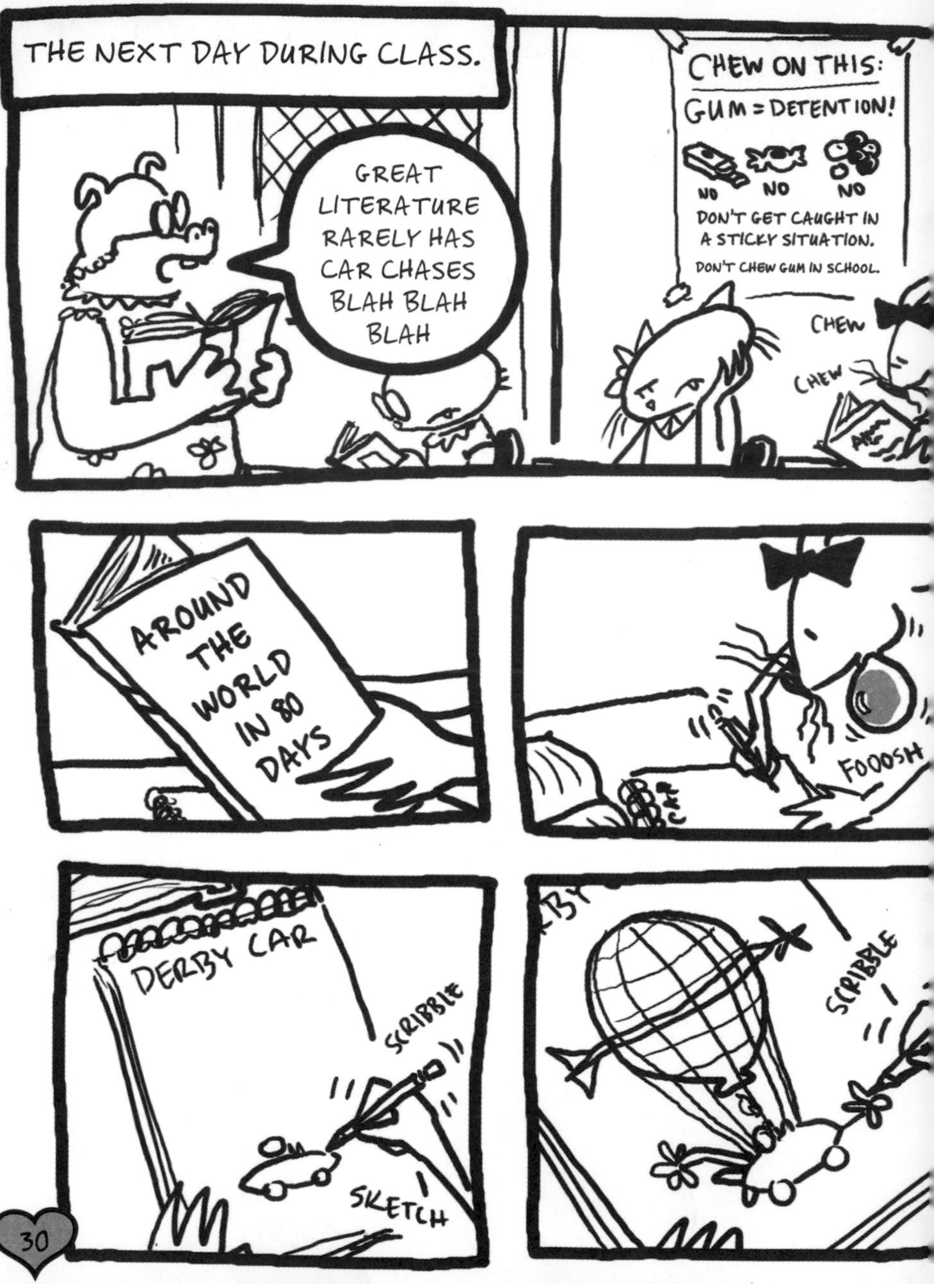
THE NEXT DAY DURING CLASS.
GREAT LITERATURE RARELY HAS CAR CHASES BLAH BLAH BLAH
CHEW ON THIS:
GUM = DETENTION!
NO NO NO
DON'T GET CAUGHT IN A STICKY SITUATION.
DON'T CHEW GUM IN SCHOOL.
CHEW
CHEW
AROUND THE WORLD IN 80 DAYS
FOOOSH
DERBY CAR
SCRIBBLE
SKETCH
SCRIBBLE

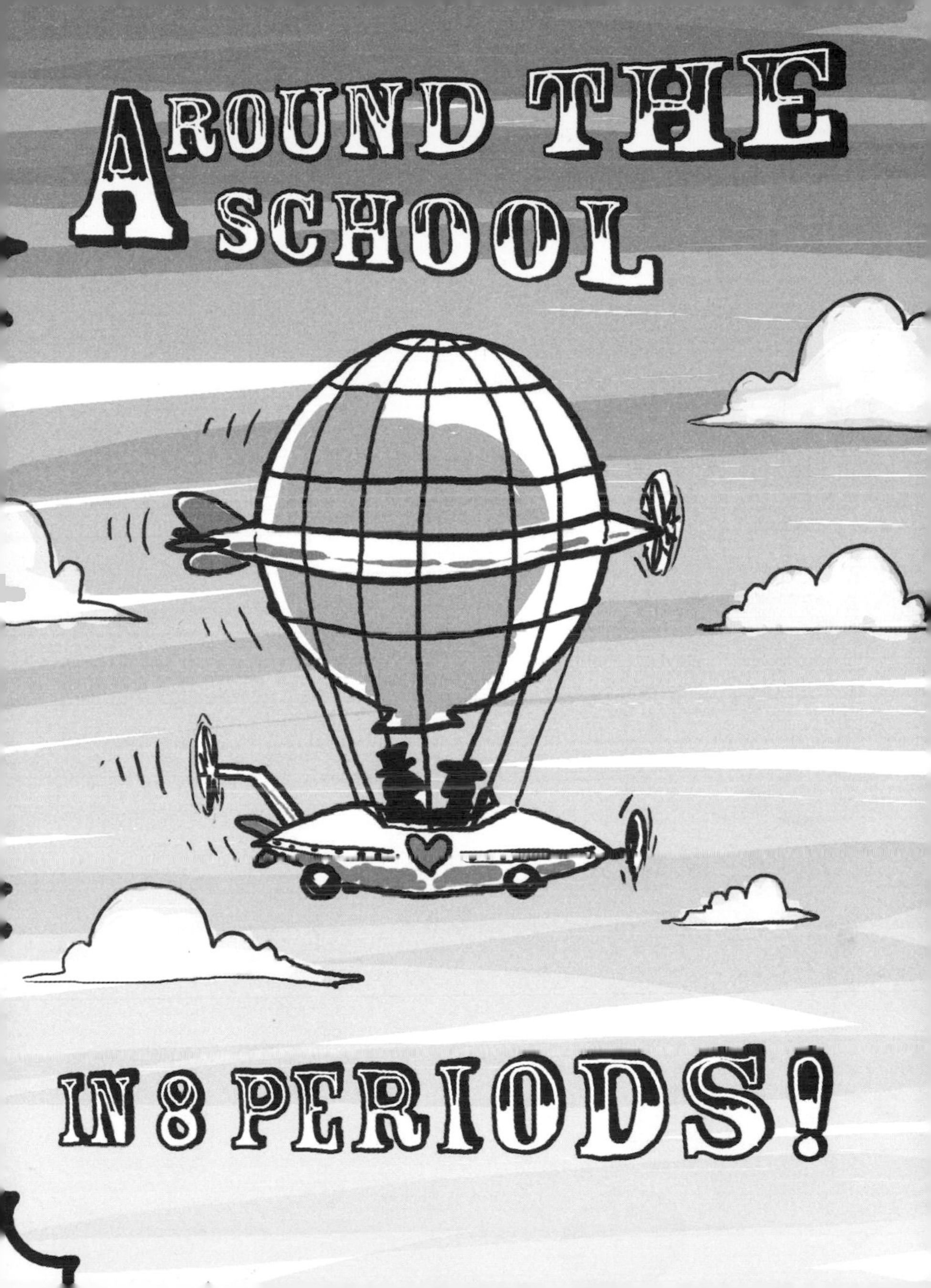
AROUND THE SCHOOL
IN 8 PERIODS!

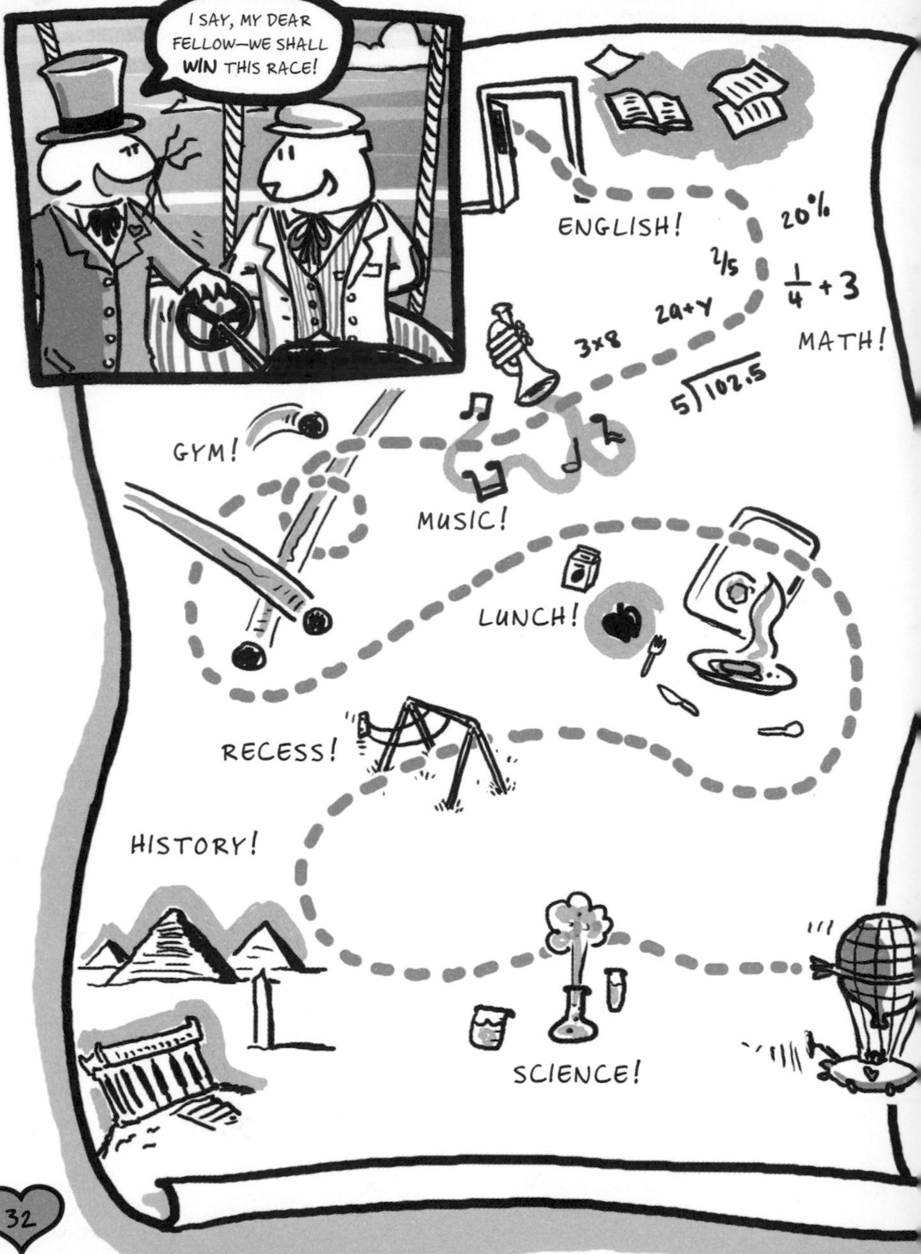
I SAY, MY DEAR FELLOW—WE SHALL **WIN** THIS RACE!
ENGLISH!
20%
2/5
1/4 + 3
2a+y
3x8
MATH!
5)102.5
GYM!
MUSIC!
LUNCH!
RECESS!
HISTORY!
SCIENCE!

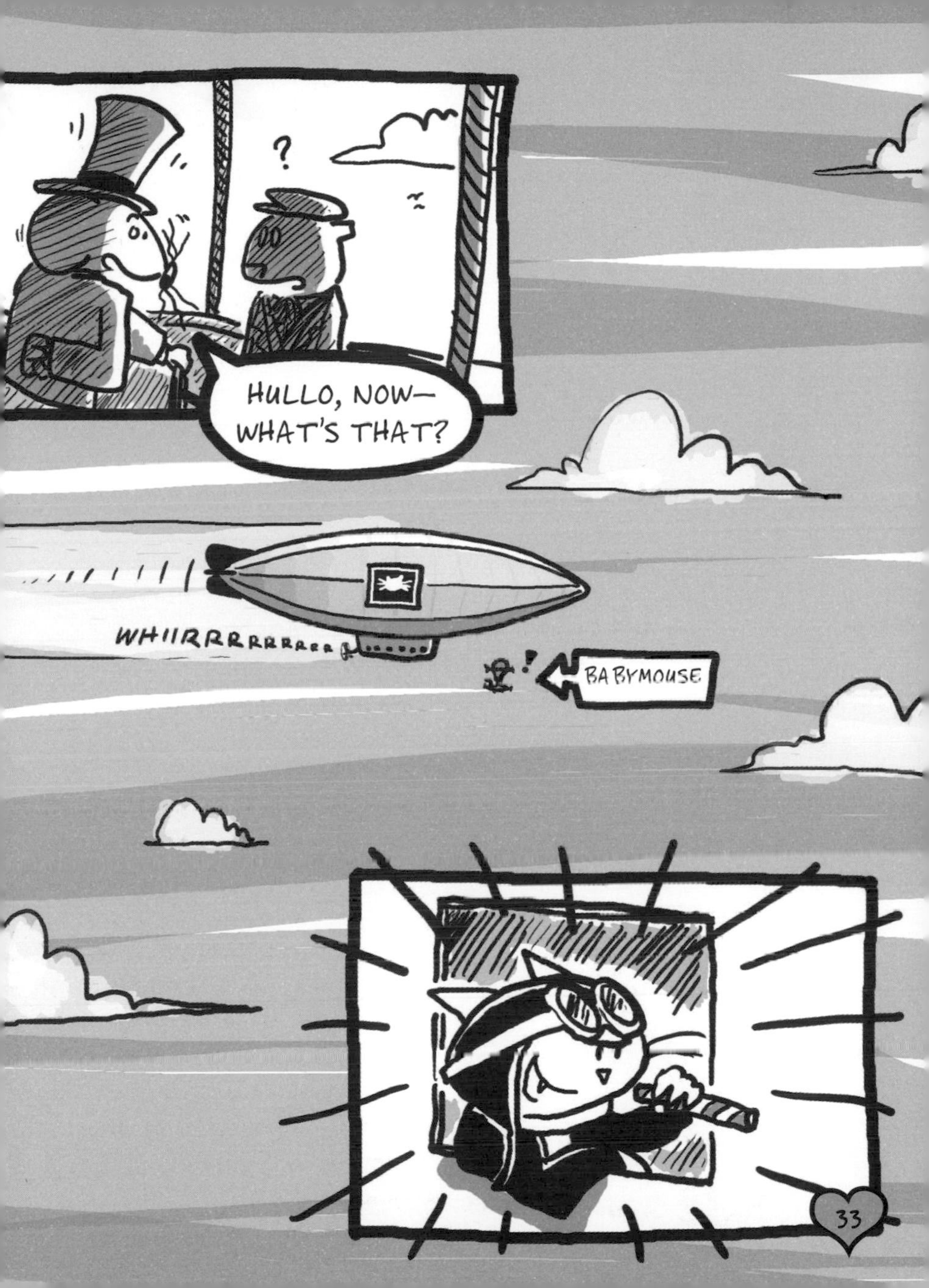
?
HULLO, NOW— WHAT'S THAT?
WHIIRRRRRRRRRRR
!
BABYMOUSE

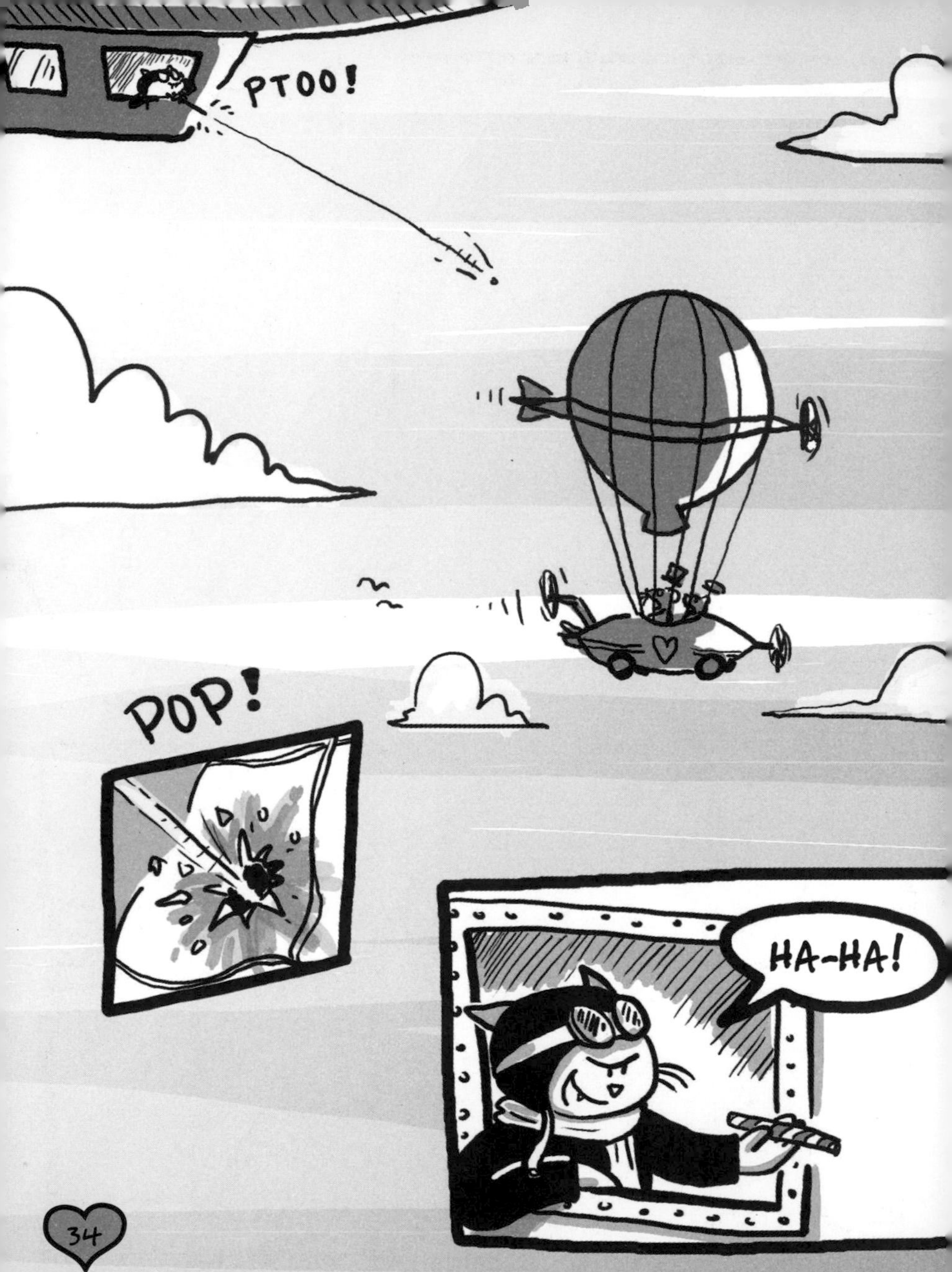
PTOO!
POP!
HA-HA!

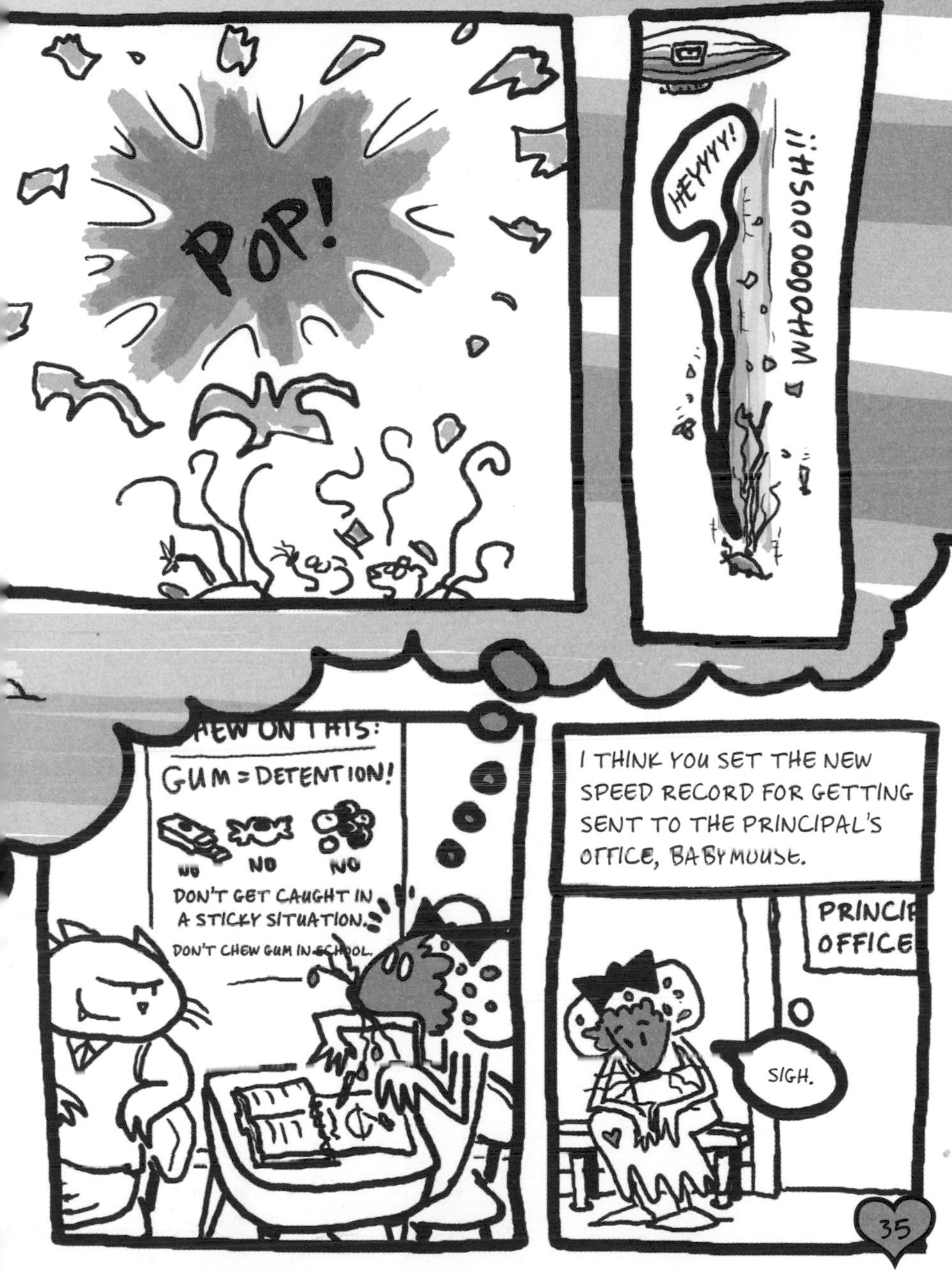
POP!
HEYYYY!
WHOOOOOOSH!!
HEW ON THIS:
GUM = DETENTION!
NO NO NO
DON'T GET CAUGHT IN A STICKY SITUATION.
DON'T CHEW GUM IN SCHOOL.
I THINK YOU SET THE NEW SPEED RECORD FOR GETTING SENT TO THE PRINCIPAL'S OFFICE, BABYMOUSE.
PRINCI
OFFICE
SIGH.

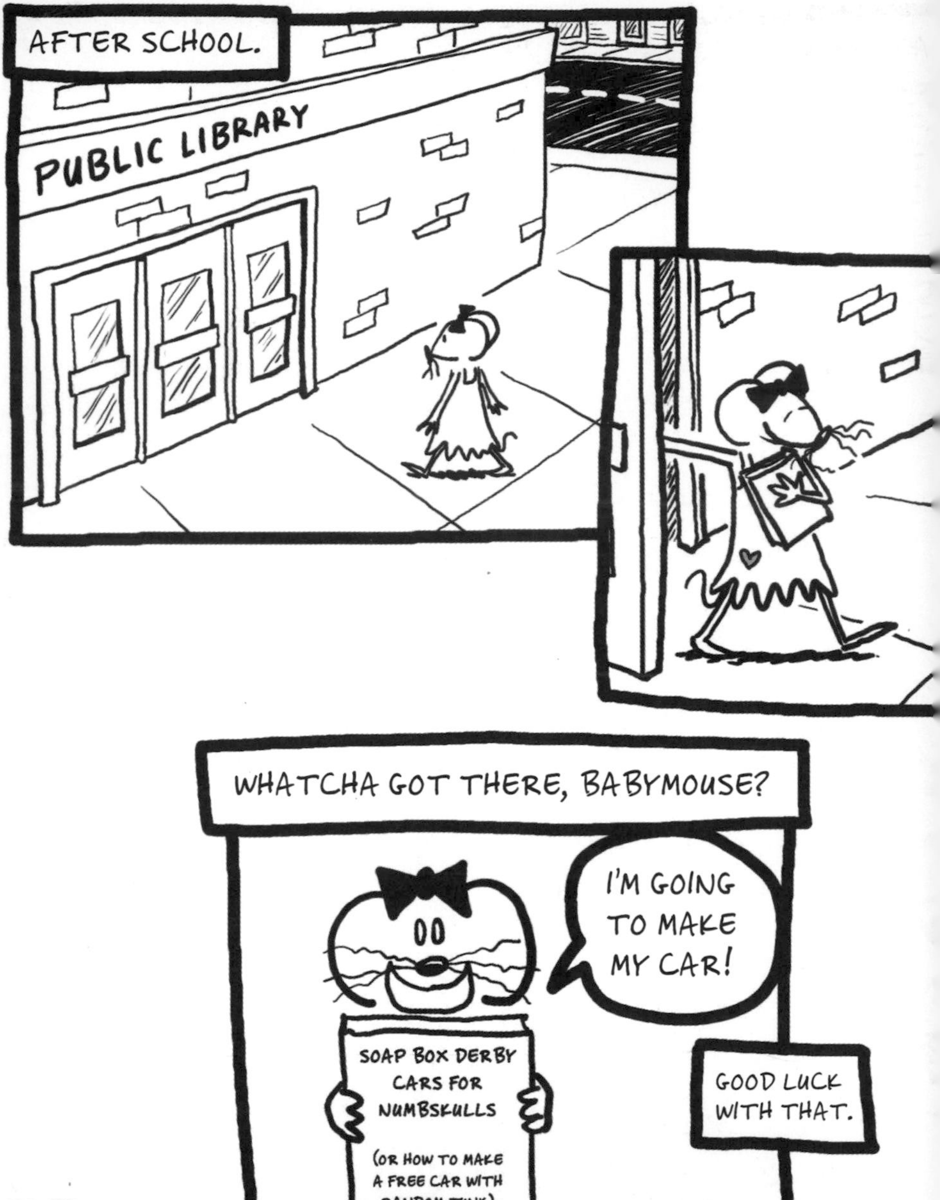
AFTER SCHOOL.
PUBLIC LIBRARY
WHATCHA GOT THERE, BABYMOUSE?
I'M GOING TO MAKE MY CAR!
SOAP BOX DERBY CARS FOR NUMBSKULLS
(OR HOW TO MAKE A FREE CAR WITH RANDOM JUNK)
GOOD LUCK WITH THAT.

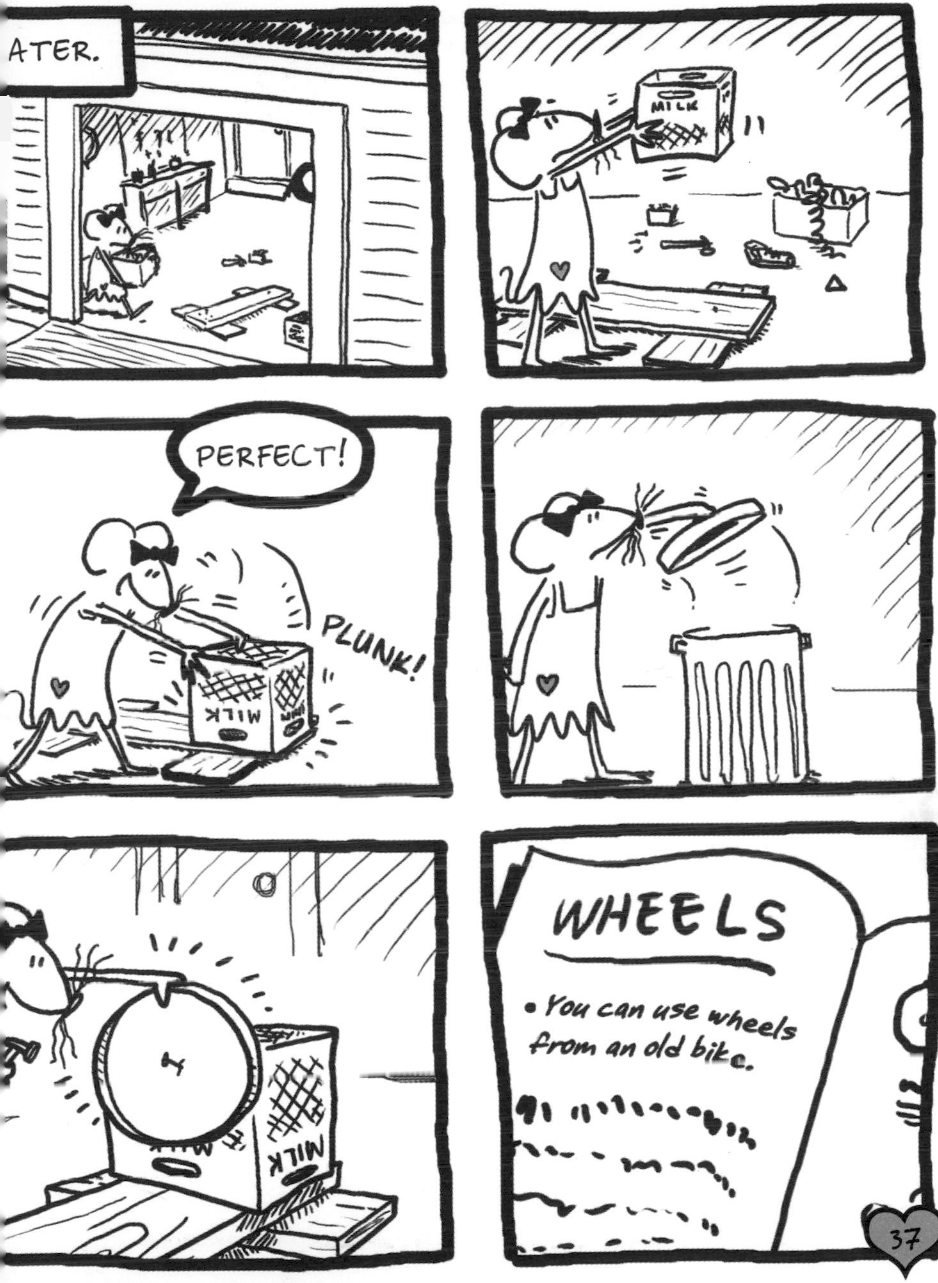
ATER.
MILK
PERFECT!
PLUNK!
WHEELS
• You can use wheels from an old bike.

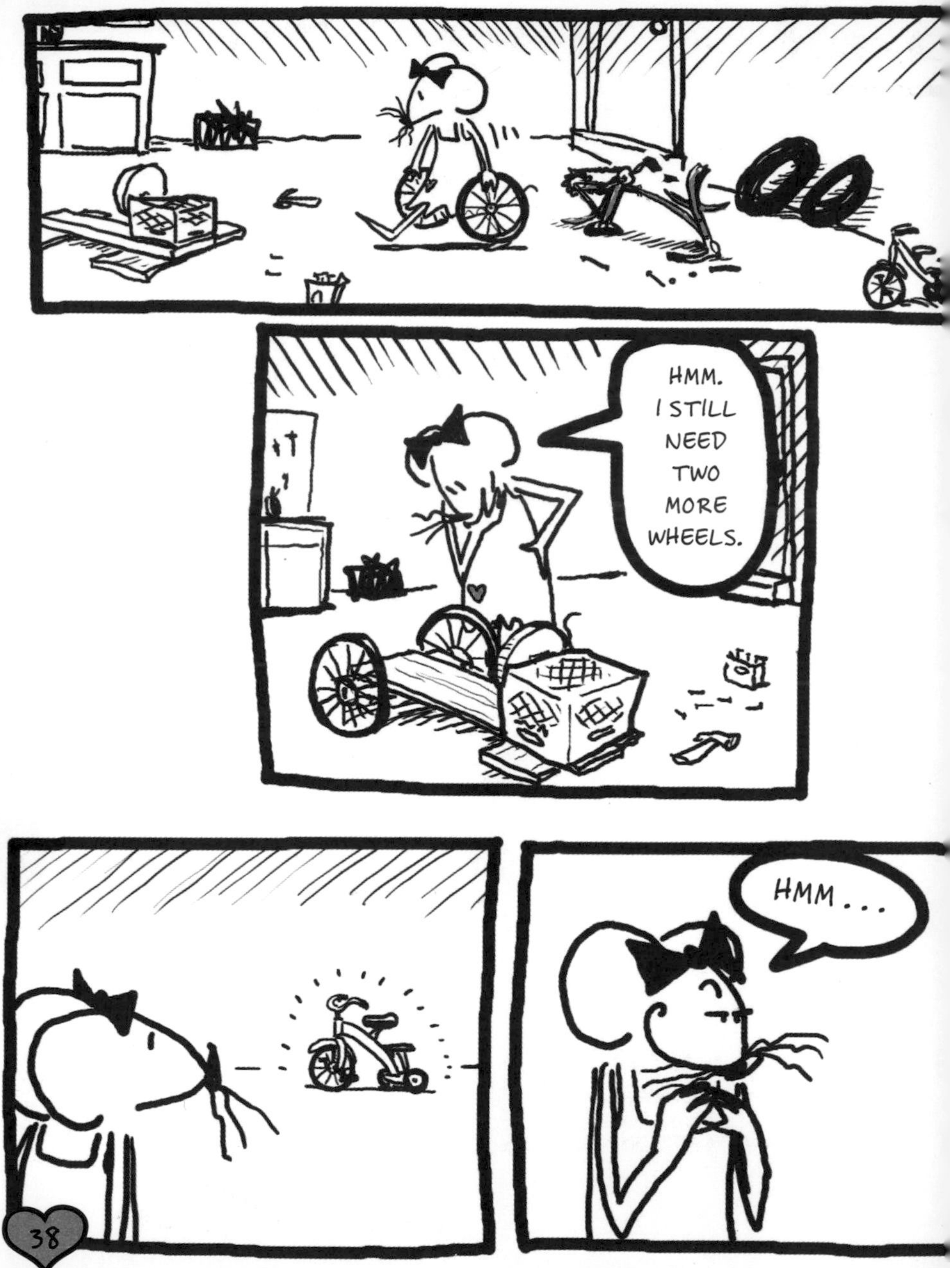
HMM.
I STILL NEED TWO MORE WHEELS.
HMM...

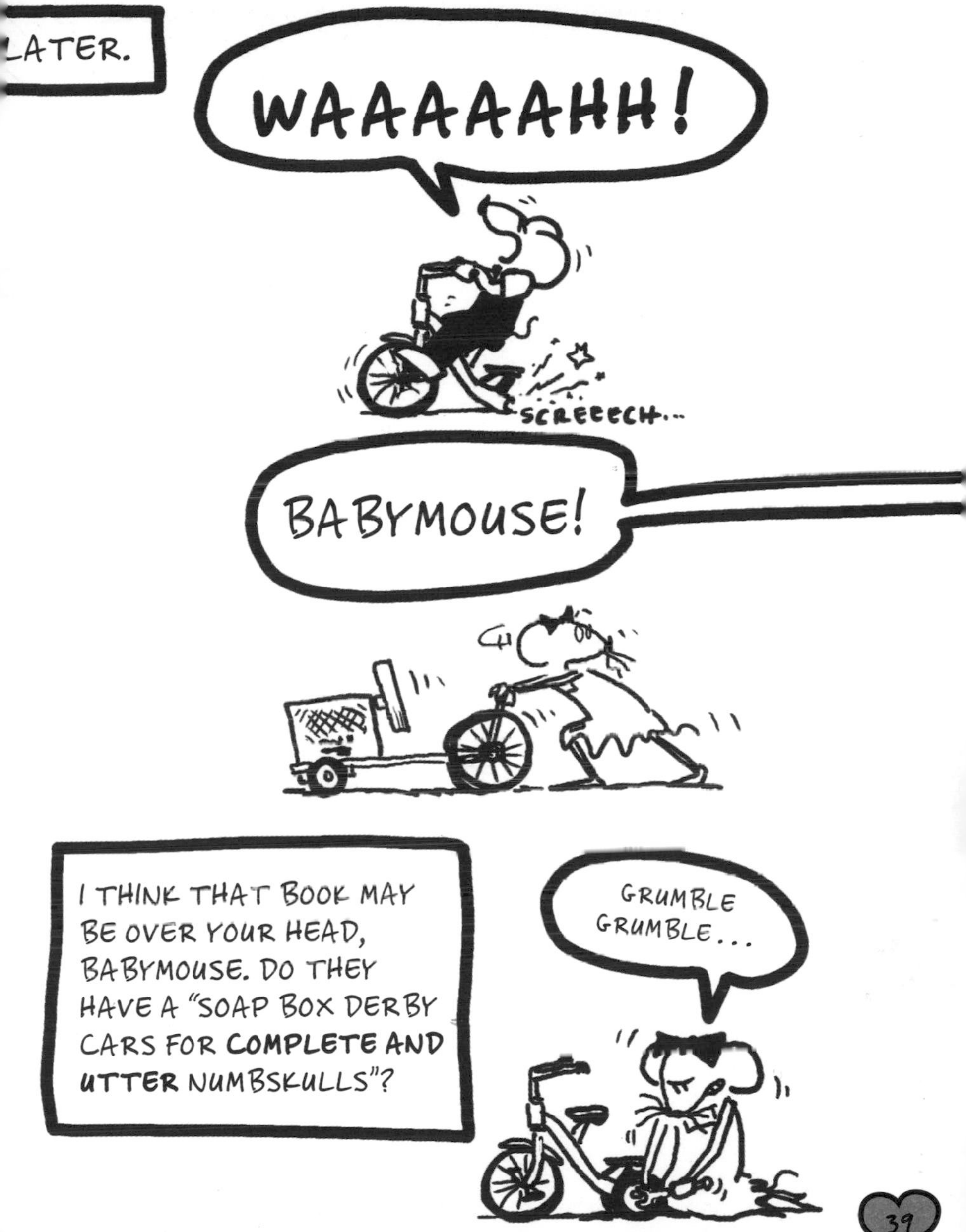
LATER.
WAAAAAHH!
SCREEECH...
BABYMOUSE!
I THINK THAT BOOK MAY BE OVER YOUR HEAD, BABYMOUSE. DO THEY HAVE A "SOAP BOX DERBY CARS FOR **COMPLETE AND UTTER** NUMBSKULLS"?
GRUMBLE GRUMBLE...

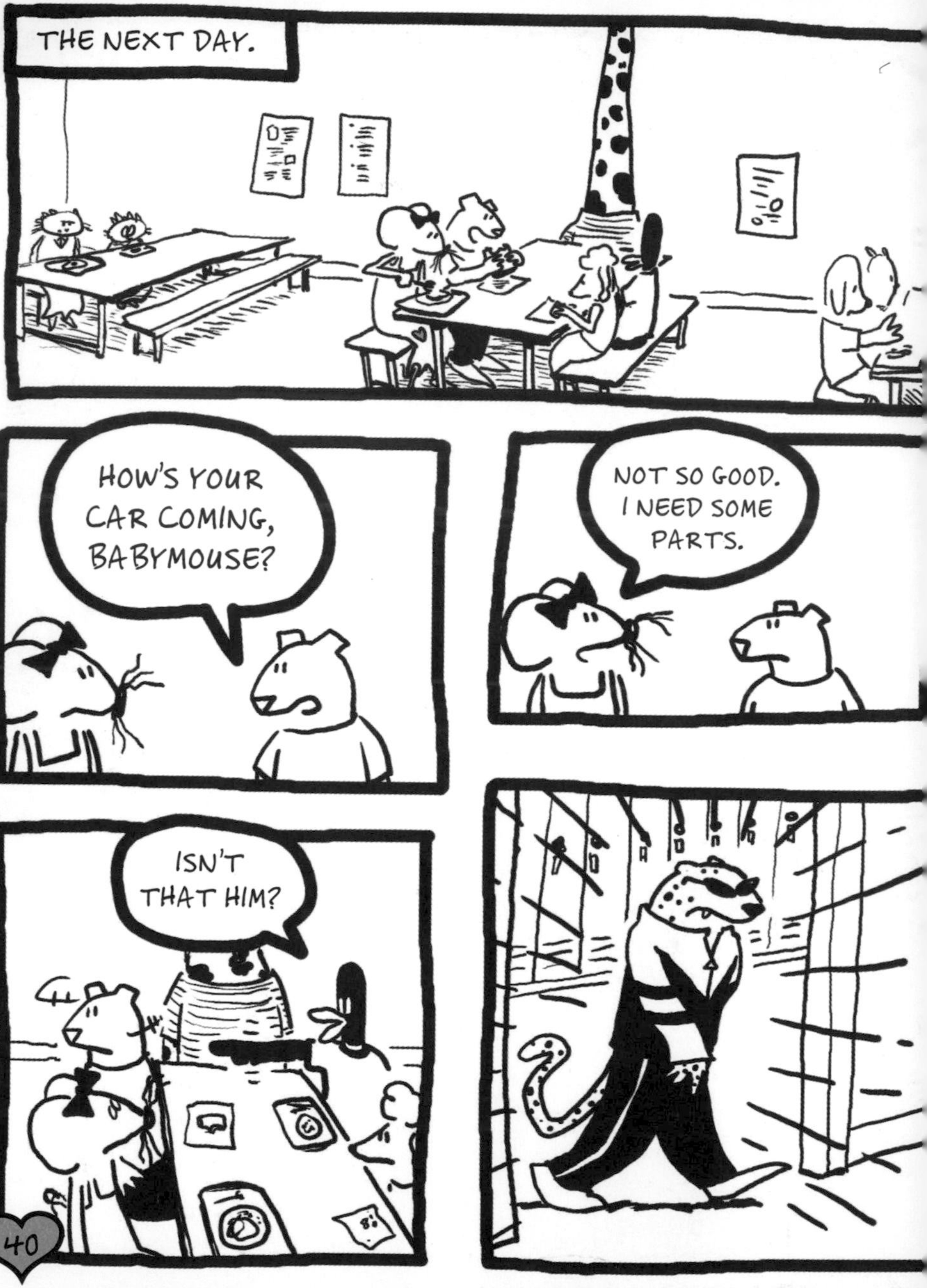
THE NEXT DAY.
HOW'S YOUR CAR COMING, BABYMOUSE?
NOT SO GOOD. I NEED SOME PARTS.
ISN'T THAT HIM?

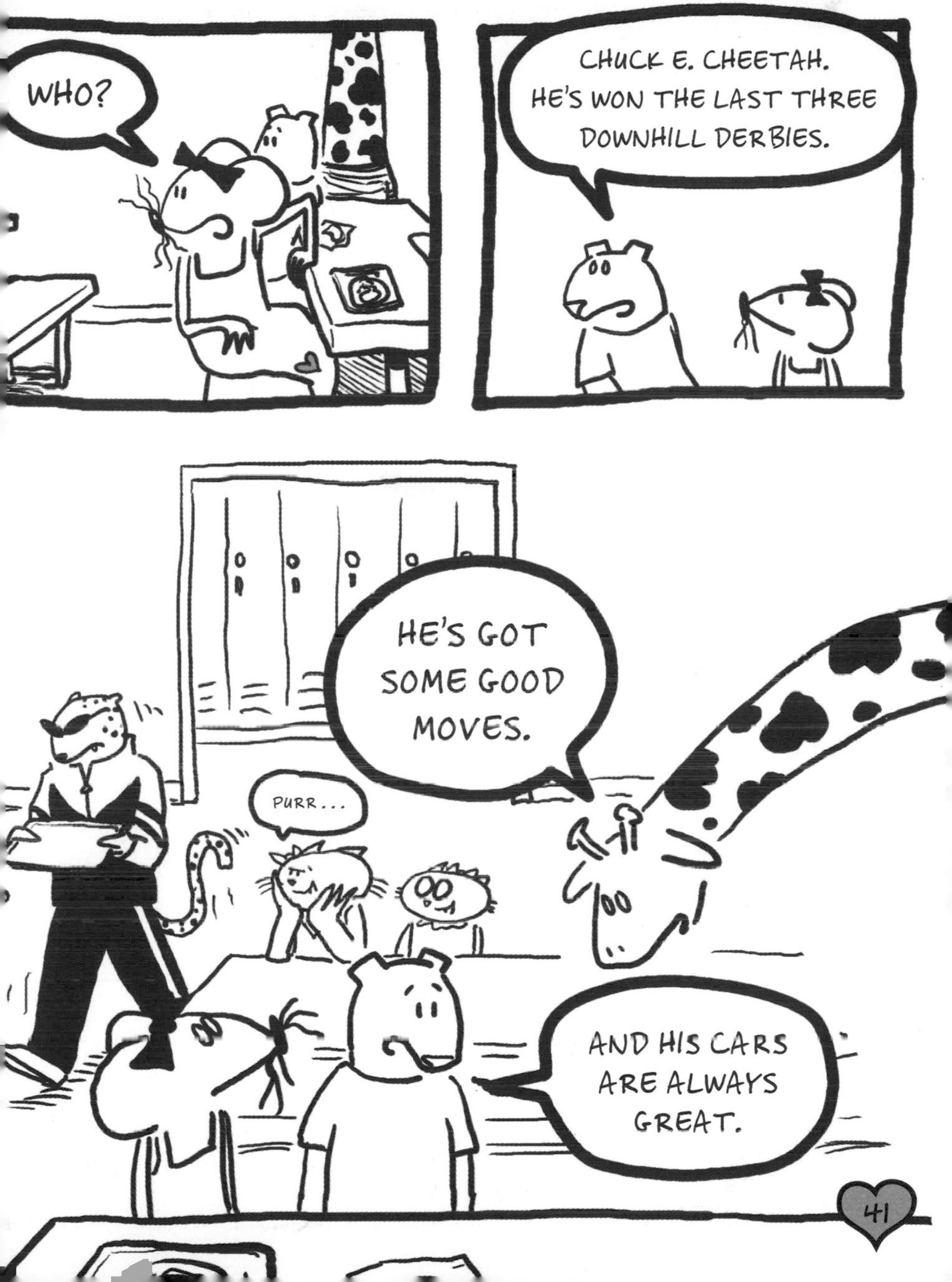
WHO?
CHUCK E. CHEETAH. HE'S WON THE LAST THREE DOWNHILL DERBIES.
HE'S GOT SOME GOOD MOVES.
PURR...
AND HIS CARS ARE ALWAYS GREAT.

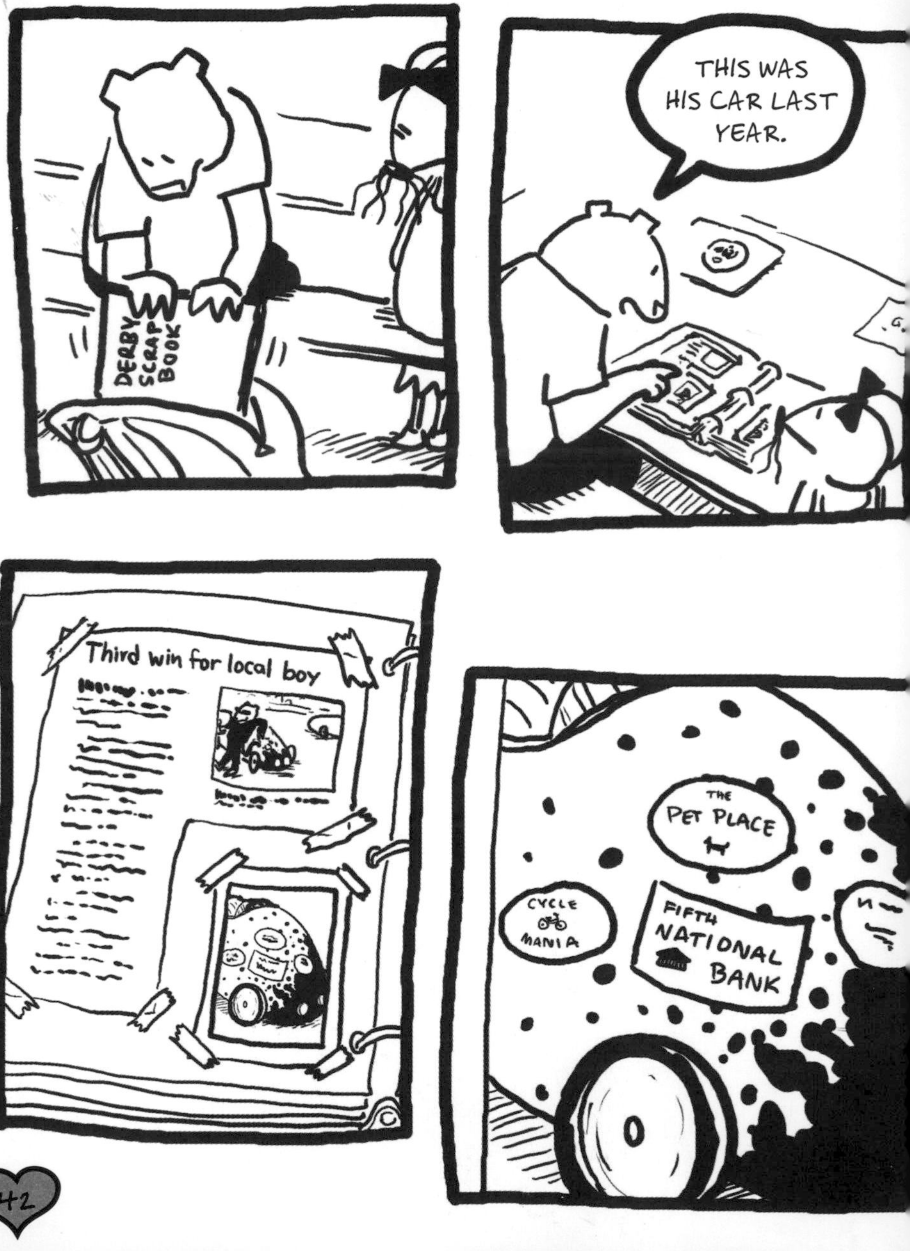
DERBY SCRAP BOOK
THIS WAS HIS CAR LAST YEAR.
Third win for local boy
THE PET PLACE
CYCLE MANIA
FIFTH NATIONAL BANK

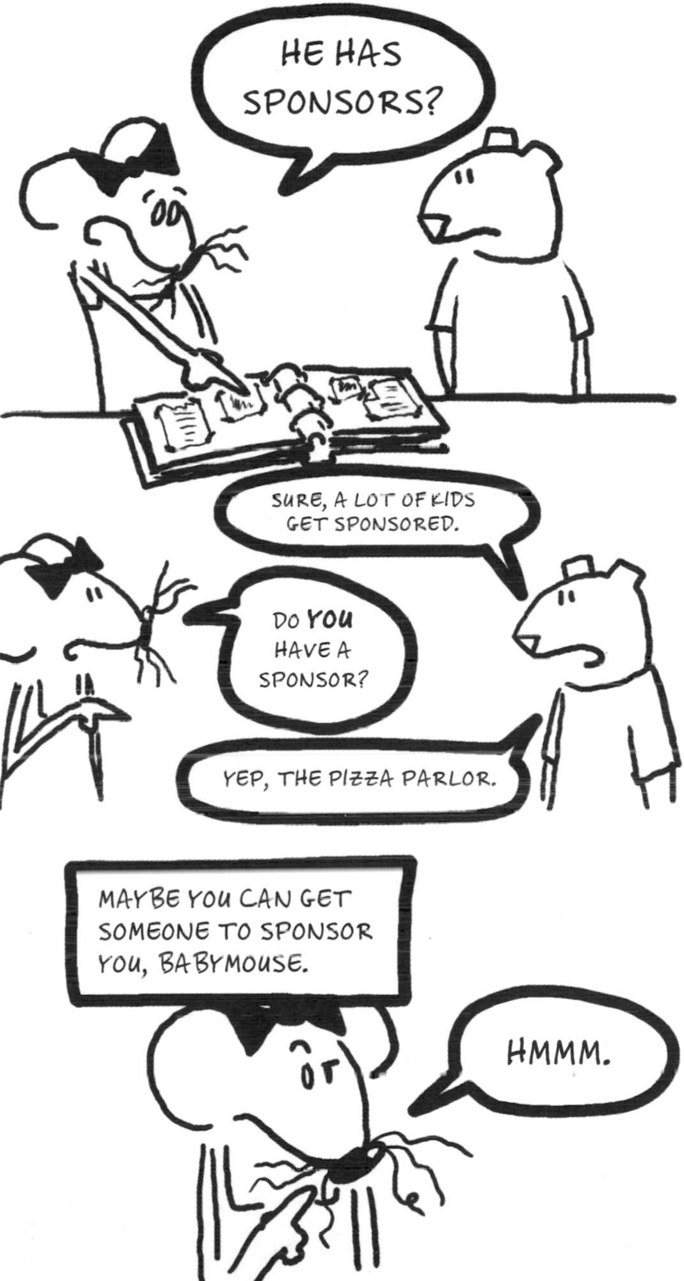
HE HAS SPONSORS?
SURE, A LOT OF KIDS GET SPONSORED.
DO **YOU** HAVE A SPONSOR?
YEP, THE PIZZA PARLOR.
MAYBE YOU CAN GET SOMEONE TO SPONSOR YOU, BABYMOUSE.
HMMM.

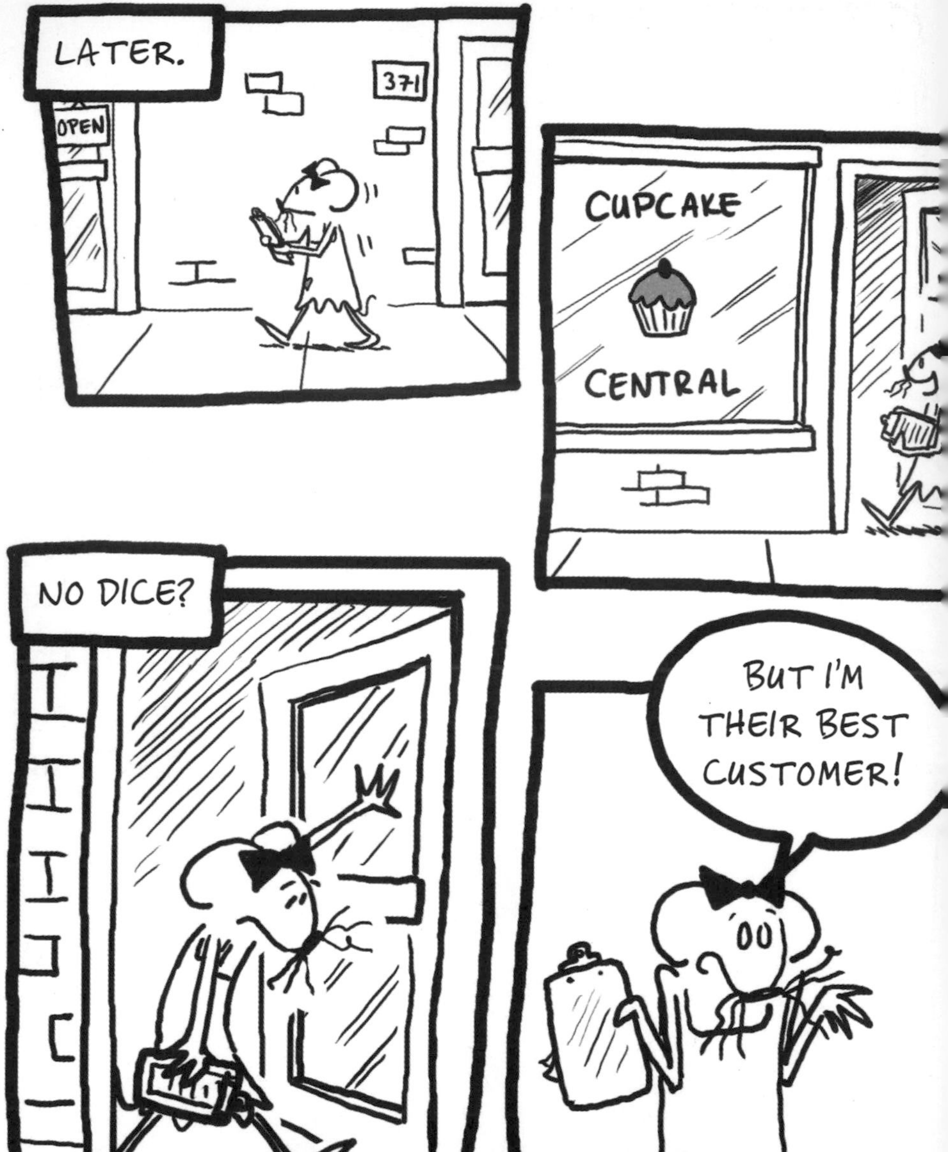
LATER.
OPEN
371
CUPCAKE
CENTRAL
NO DICE?
BUT I'M THEIR BEST CUSTOMER!

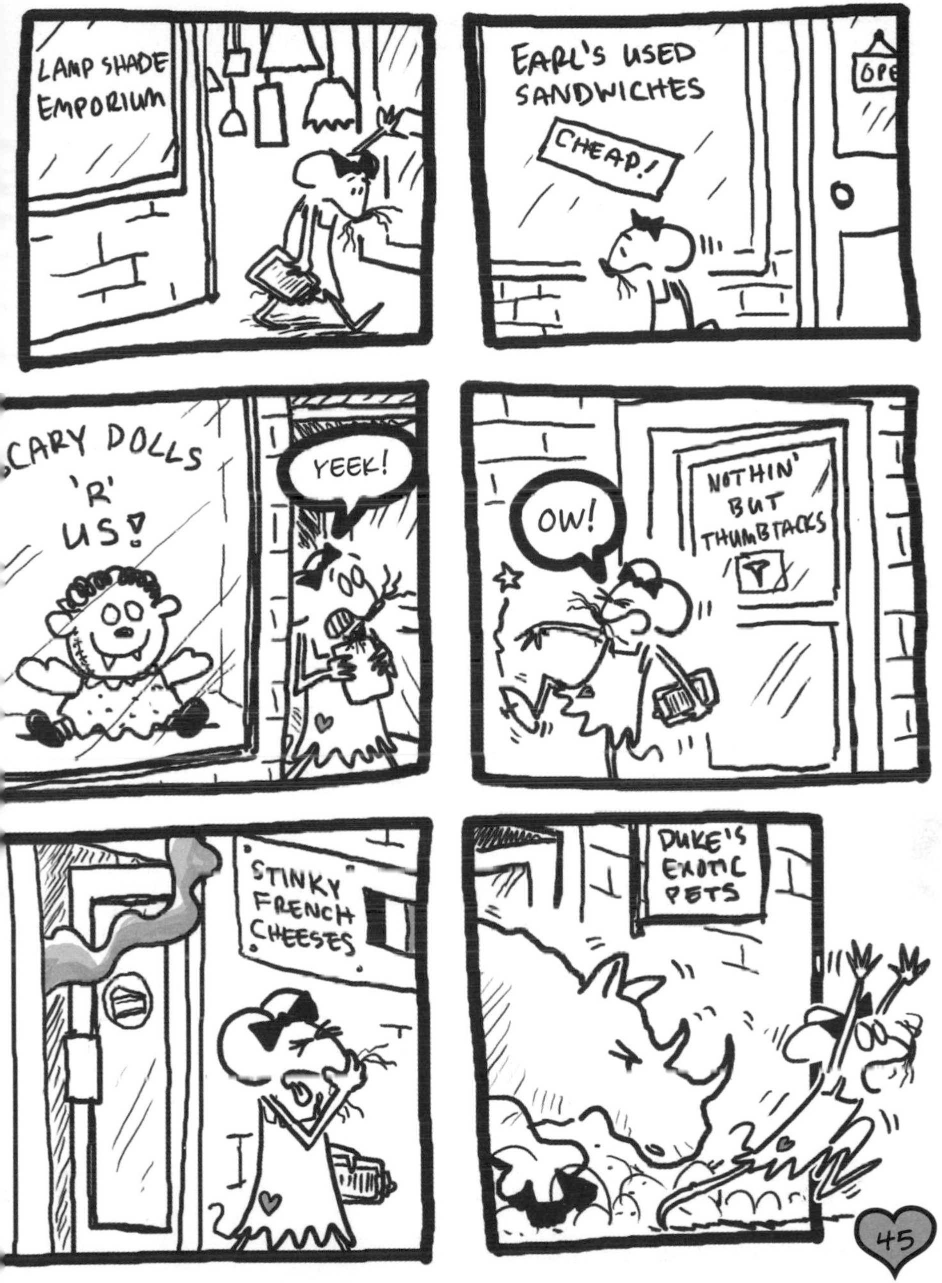
LAMP SHADE EMPORIUM
EARL'S USED SANDWICHES
CHEAP!
SCARY DOLLS 'R' US!
YEEK!
NOTHIN' BUT THUMBTACKS
OW!
STINKY FRENCH CHEESES
DUKE'S EXOTIC PETS

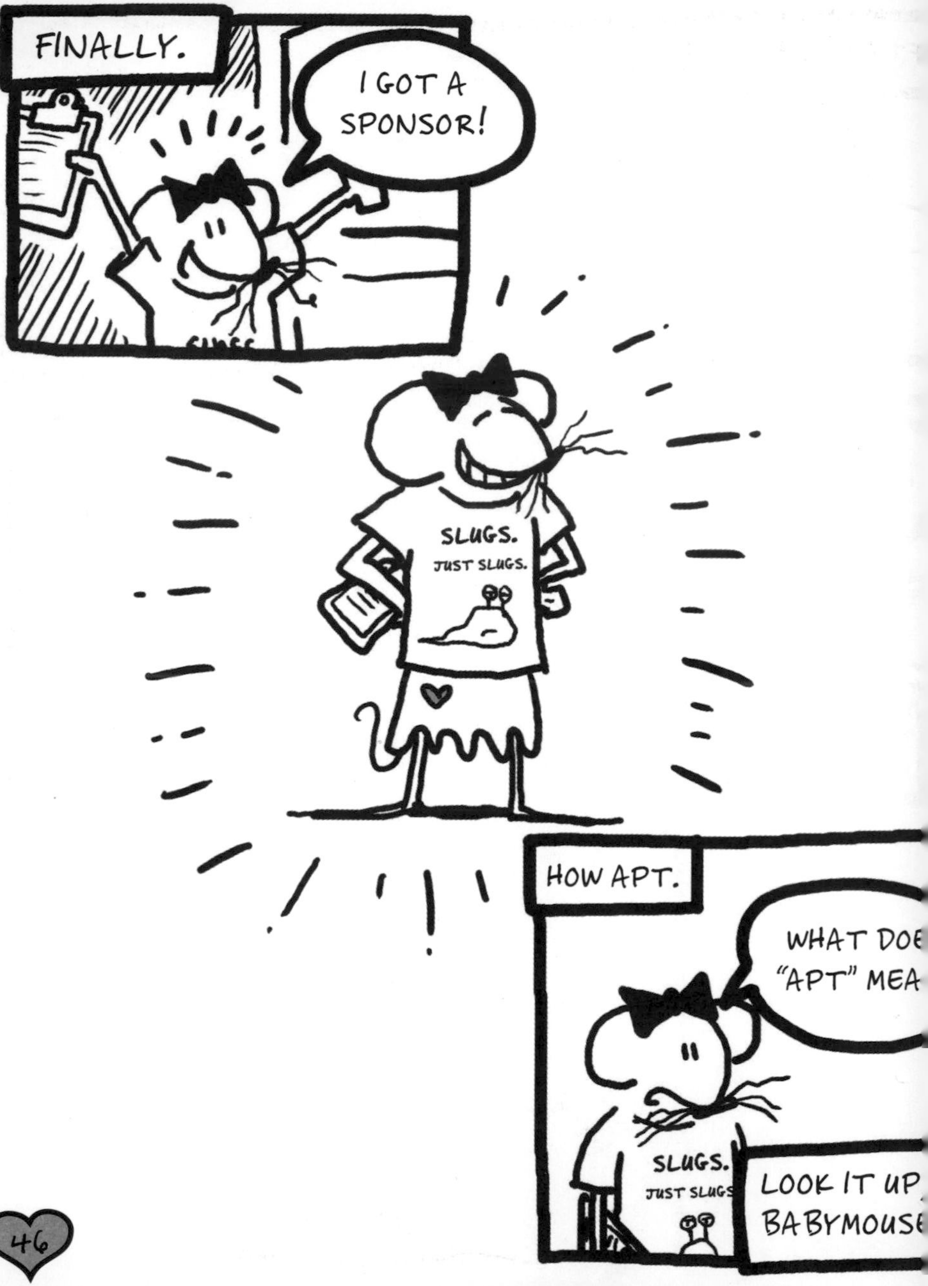
FINALLY.
I GOT A SPONSOR!
SLUGS.
JUST SLUGS.
HOW APT.
WHAT DOE
"APT" MEA
SLUGS.
JUST SLUGS
LOOK IT UP,
BABYMOUSE

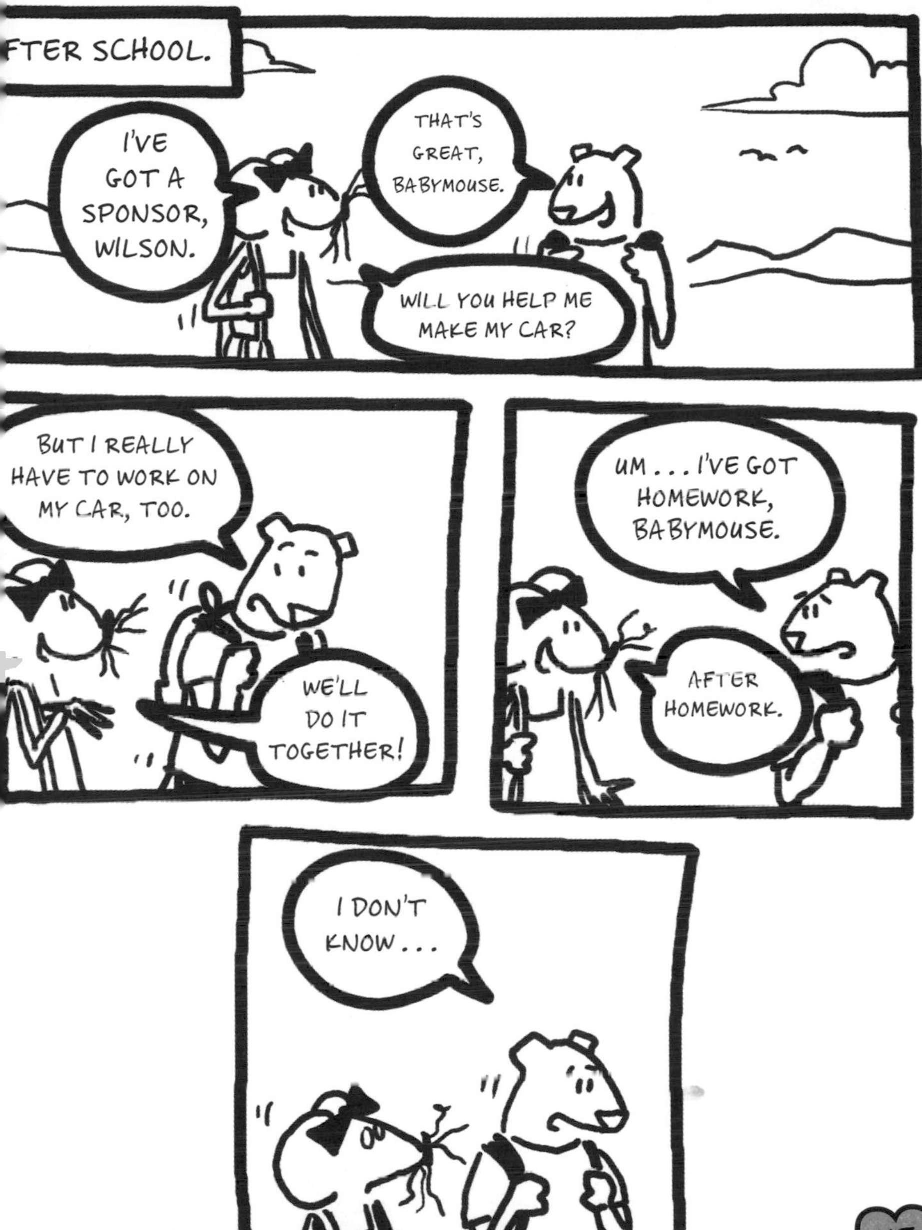
FTER SCHOOL.
I'VE GOT A SPONSOR, WILSON.
THAT'S GREAT, BABYMOUSE.
WILL YOU HELP ME MAKE MY CAR?
BUT I REALLY HAVE TO WORK ON MY CAR, TOO.
WE'LL DO IT TOGETHER!
UM . . . I'VE GOT HOMEWORK, BABYMOUSE.
AFTER HOMEWORK.
I DON'T KNOW . . .

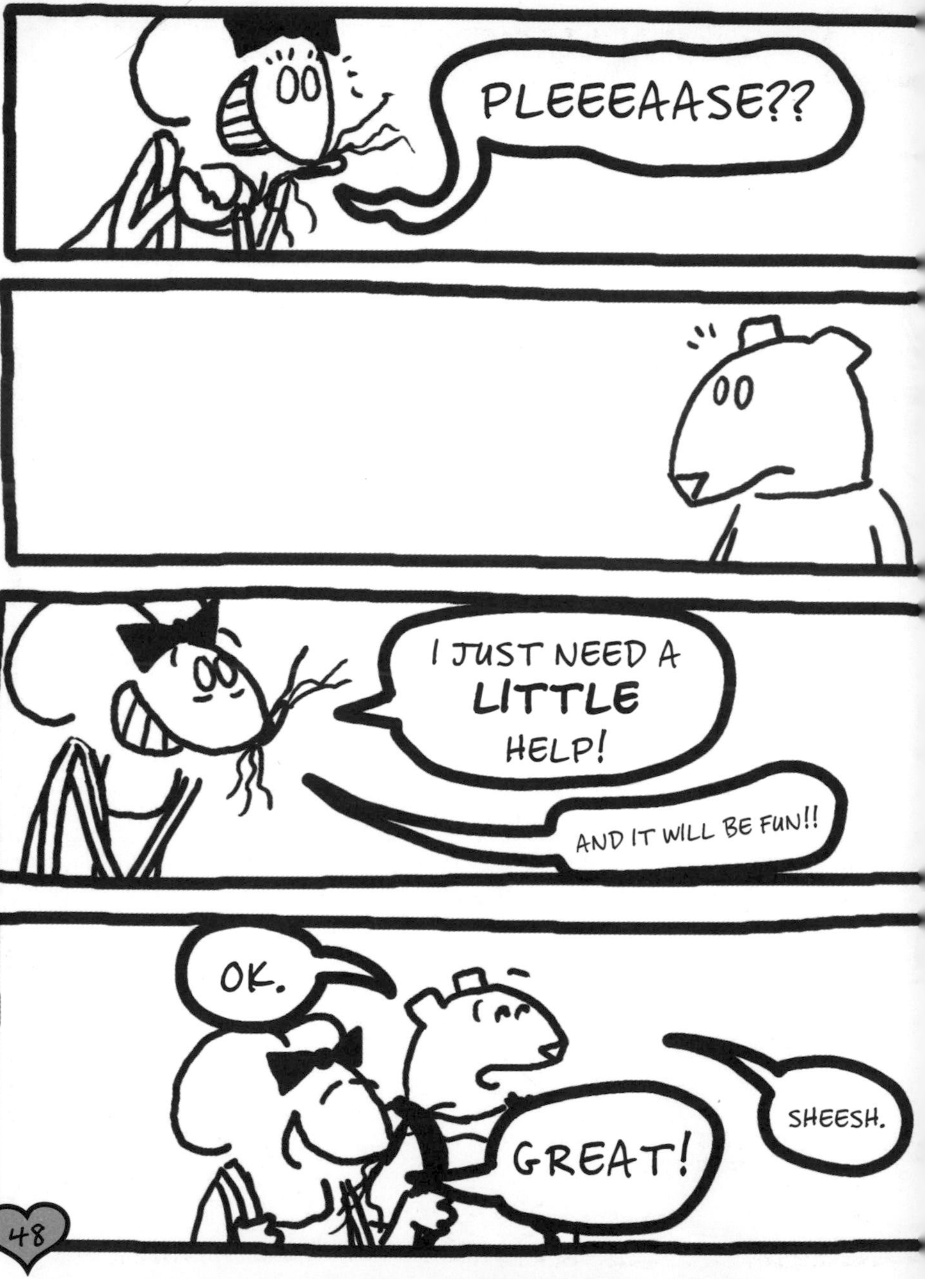
PLEEEAASE??
I JUST NEED A LITTLE HELP!
AND IT WILL BE FUN!!
OK.
GREAT!
SHEESH.

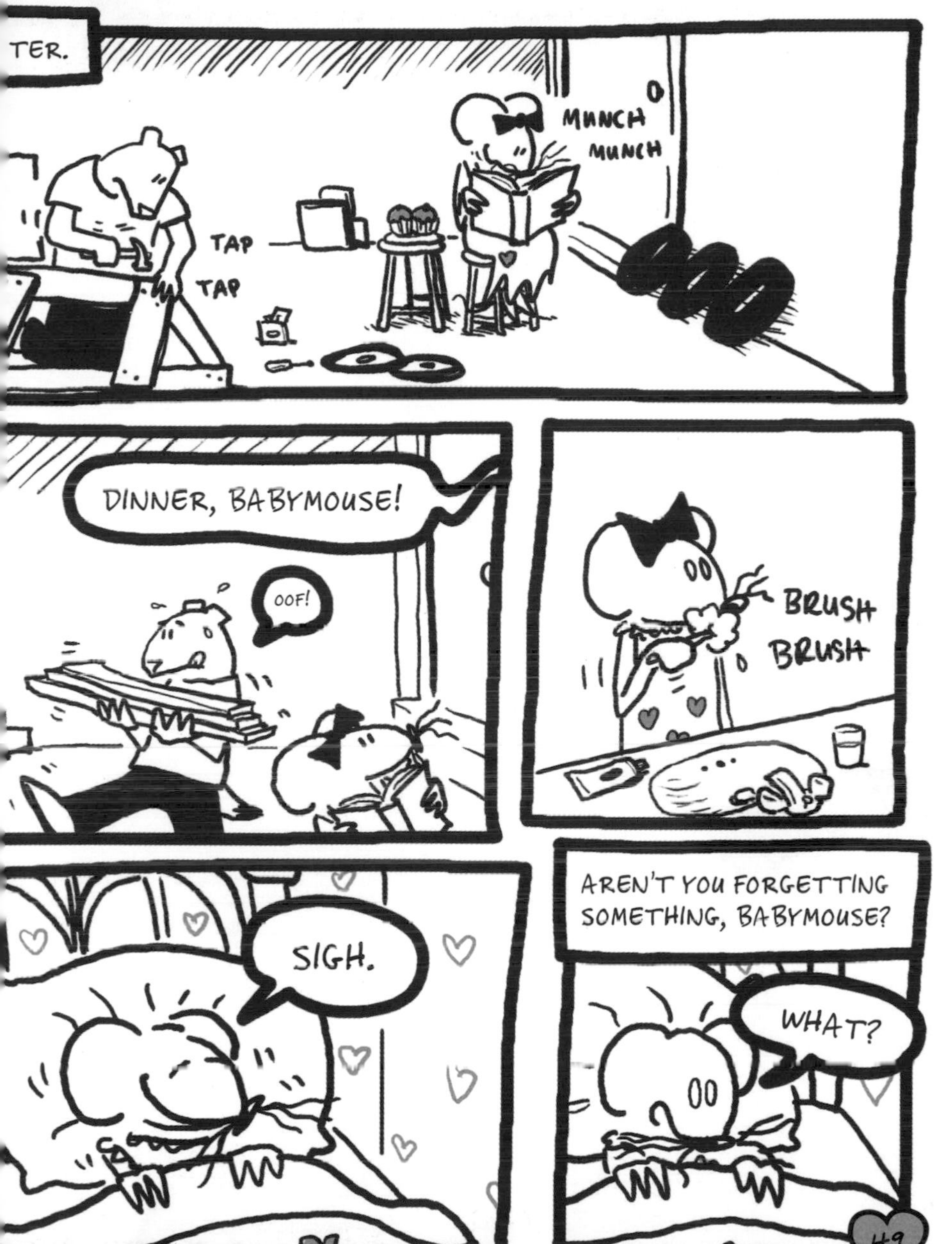

TER.
TAP
TAP
MUNCH
MUNCH
DINNER, BABYMOUSE!
OOF!
BRUSH
BRUSH
SIGH.
AREN'T YOU FORGETTING SOMETHING, BABYMOUSE?
WHAT?

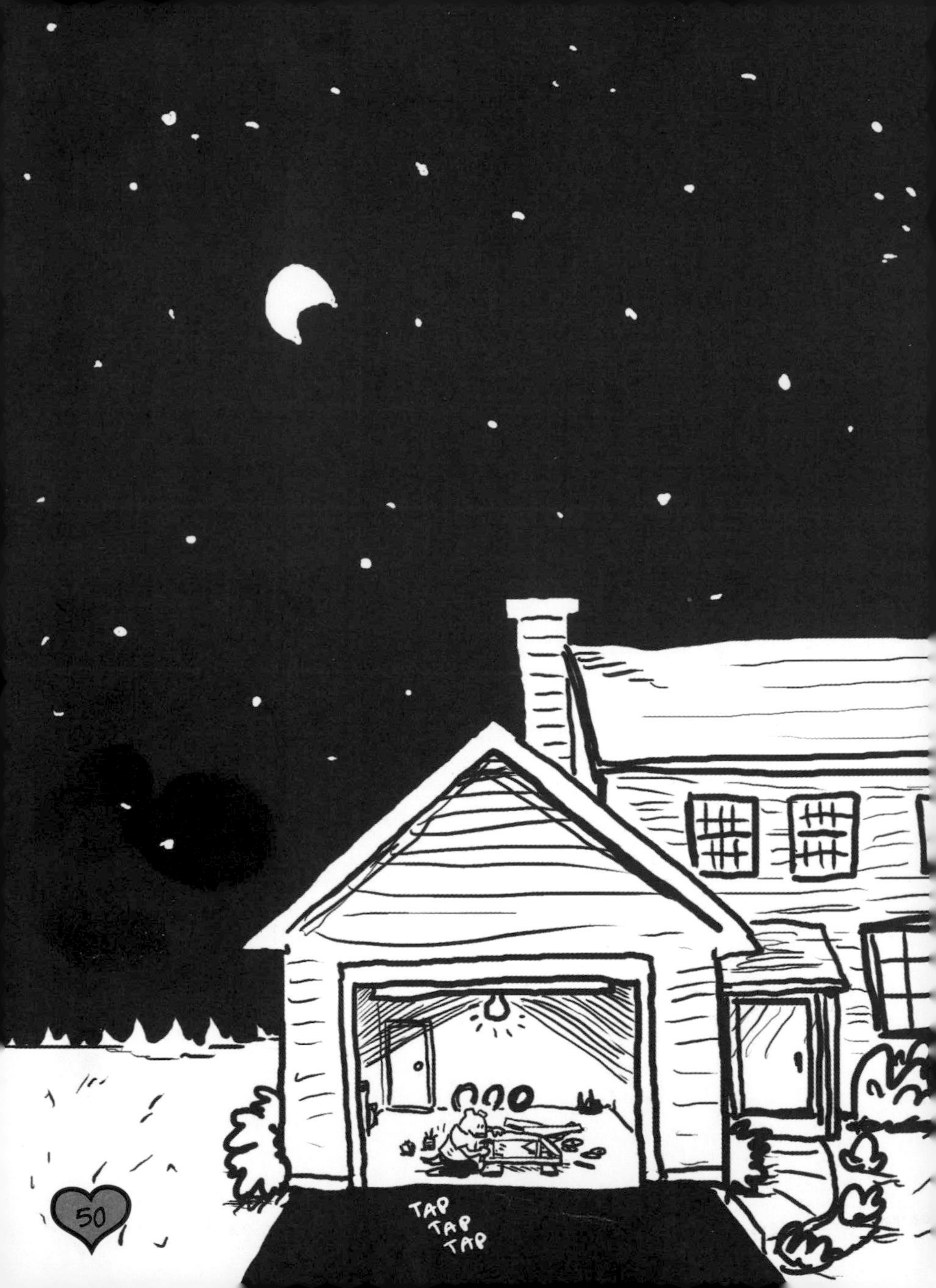
TAP
TAP
TAP

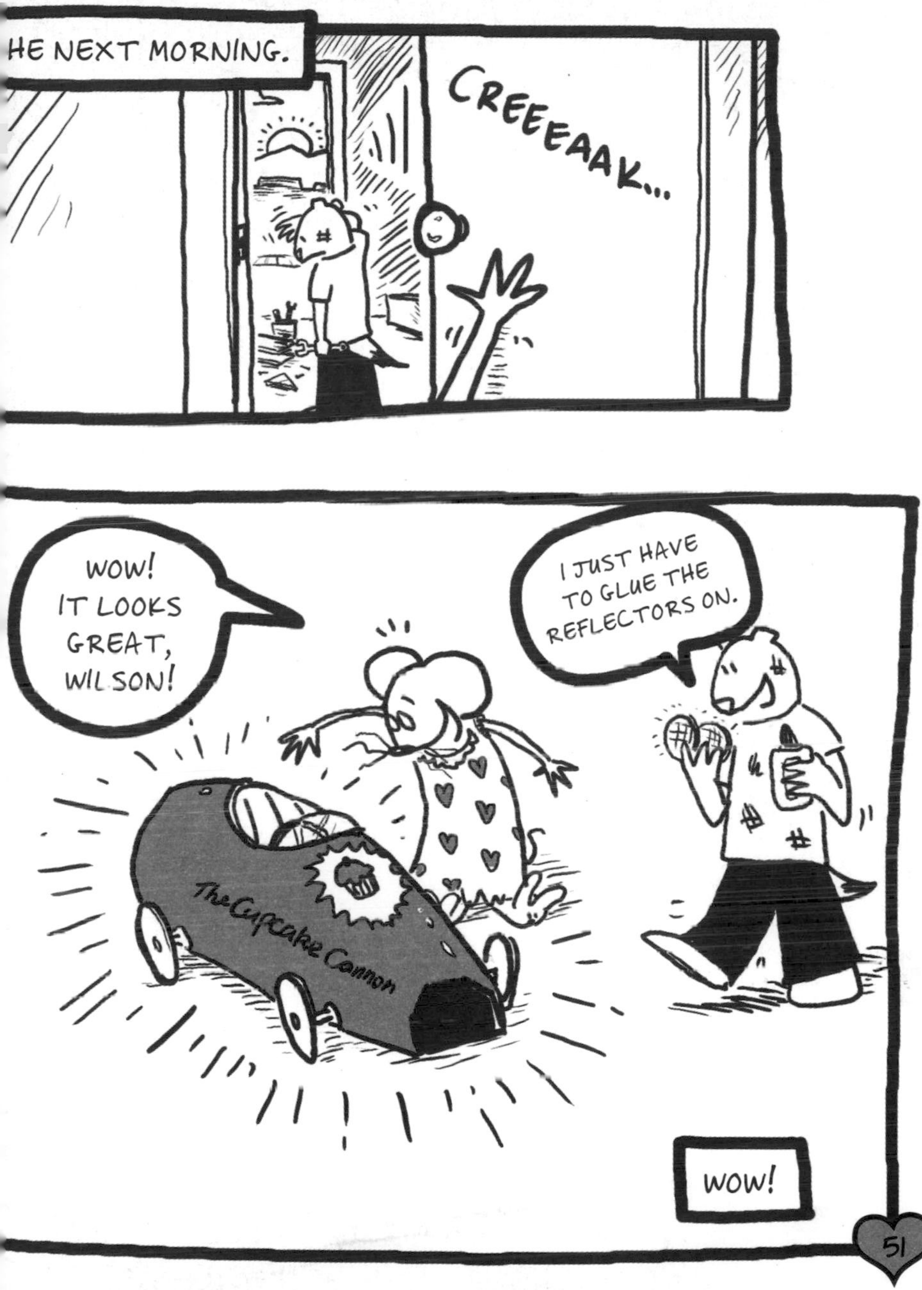
HE NEXT MORNING.
CREEEAAAK...
WOW! IT LOOKS GREAT, WILSON!
I JUST HAVE TO GLUE THE REFLECTORS ON.
The Cupcake Cannon
WOW!

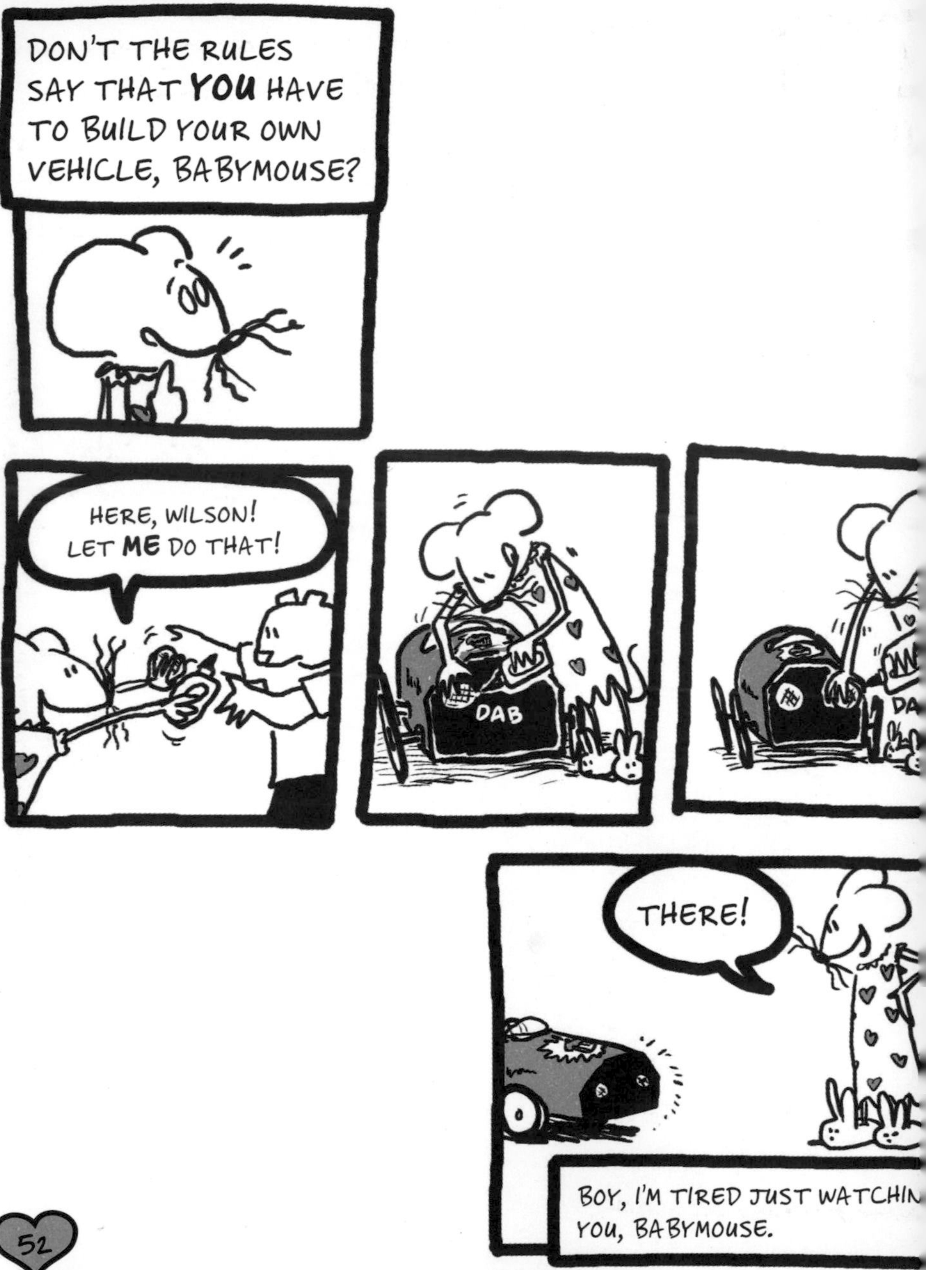
DON'T THE RULES SAY THAT **YOU** HAVE TO BUILD YOUR OWN VEHICLE, BABYMOUSE?
HERE, WILSON! LET **ME** DO THAT!
DAB
THERE!
BOY, I'M TIRED JUST WATCHIN
YOU, BABYMOUSE.

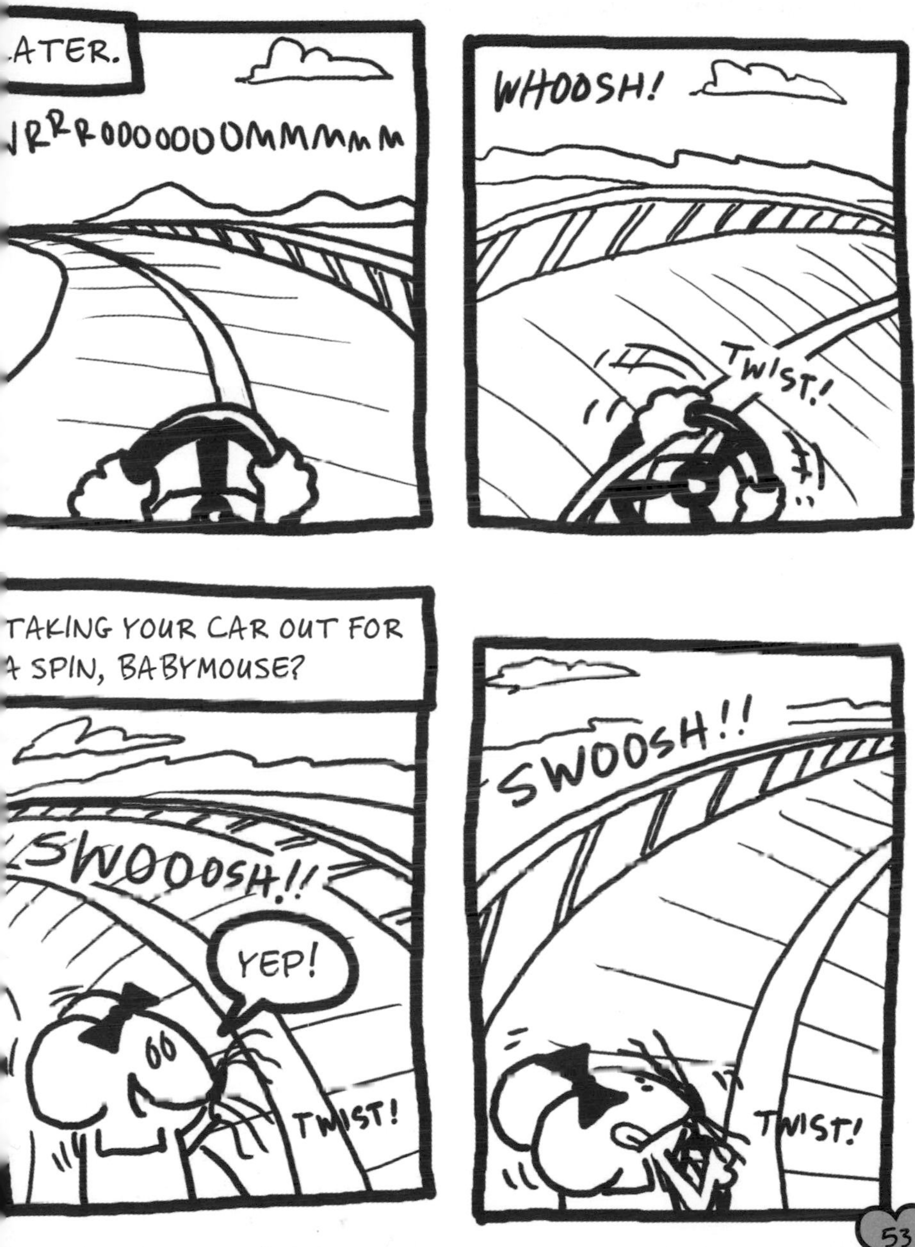

LATER.
VRRRROOOOOOOOMMMMMM
WHOOSH!
TWIST!
TAKING YOUR CAR OUT FOR A SPIN, BABYMOUSE?
SWOOOOSH!!
YEP!
TWIST!
SWOOSH!!
TWIST!

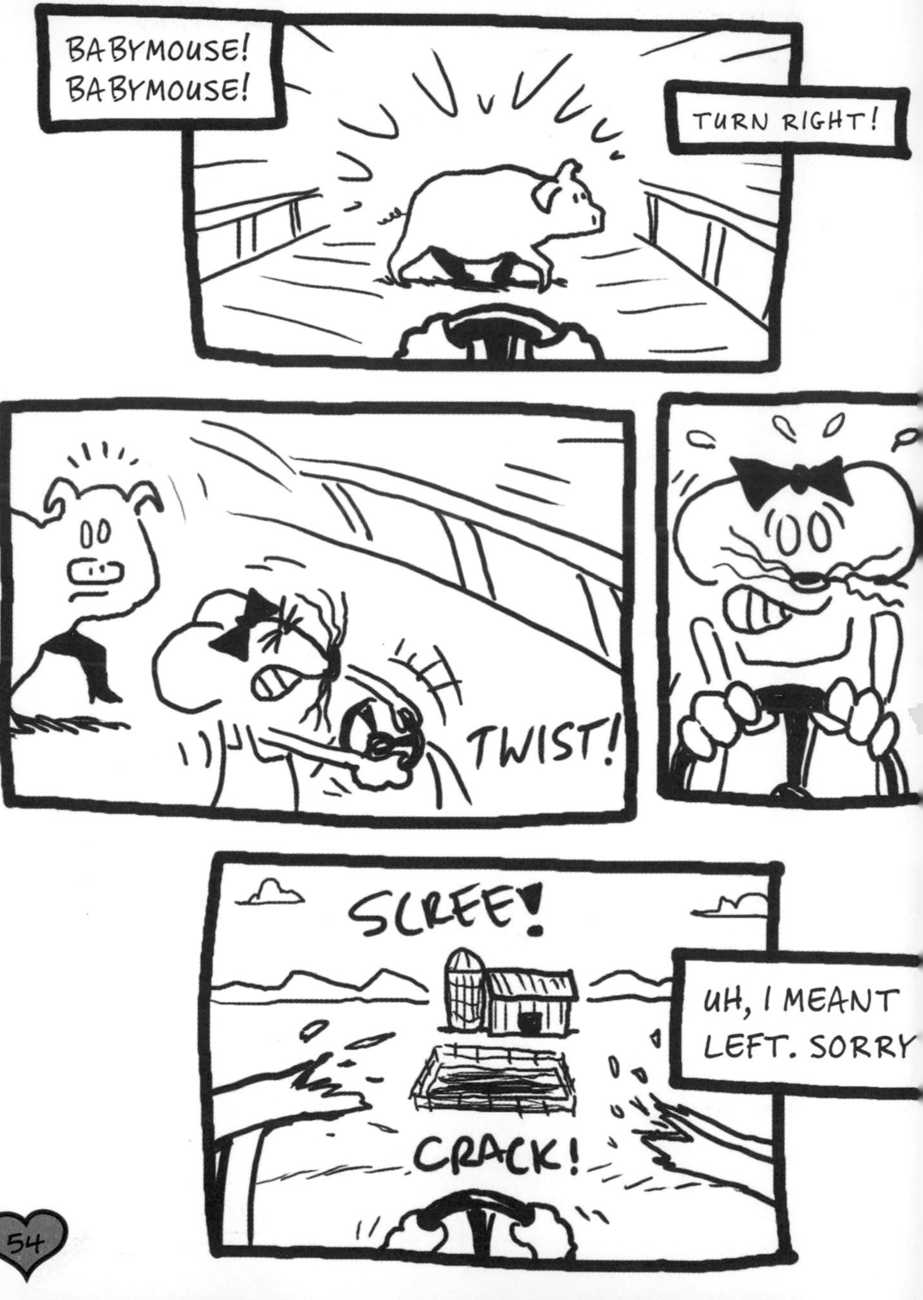
BABYMOUSE! BABYMOUSE!
TURN RIGHT!
TWIST!
SCREE!
UH, I MEANT LEFT. SORRY
CRACK!

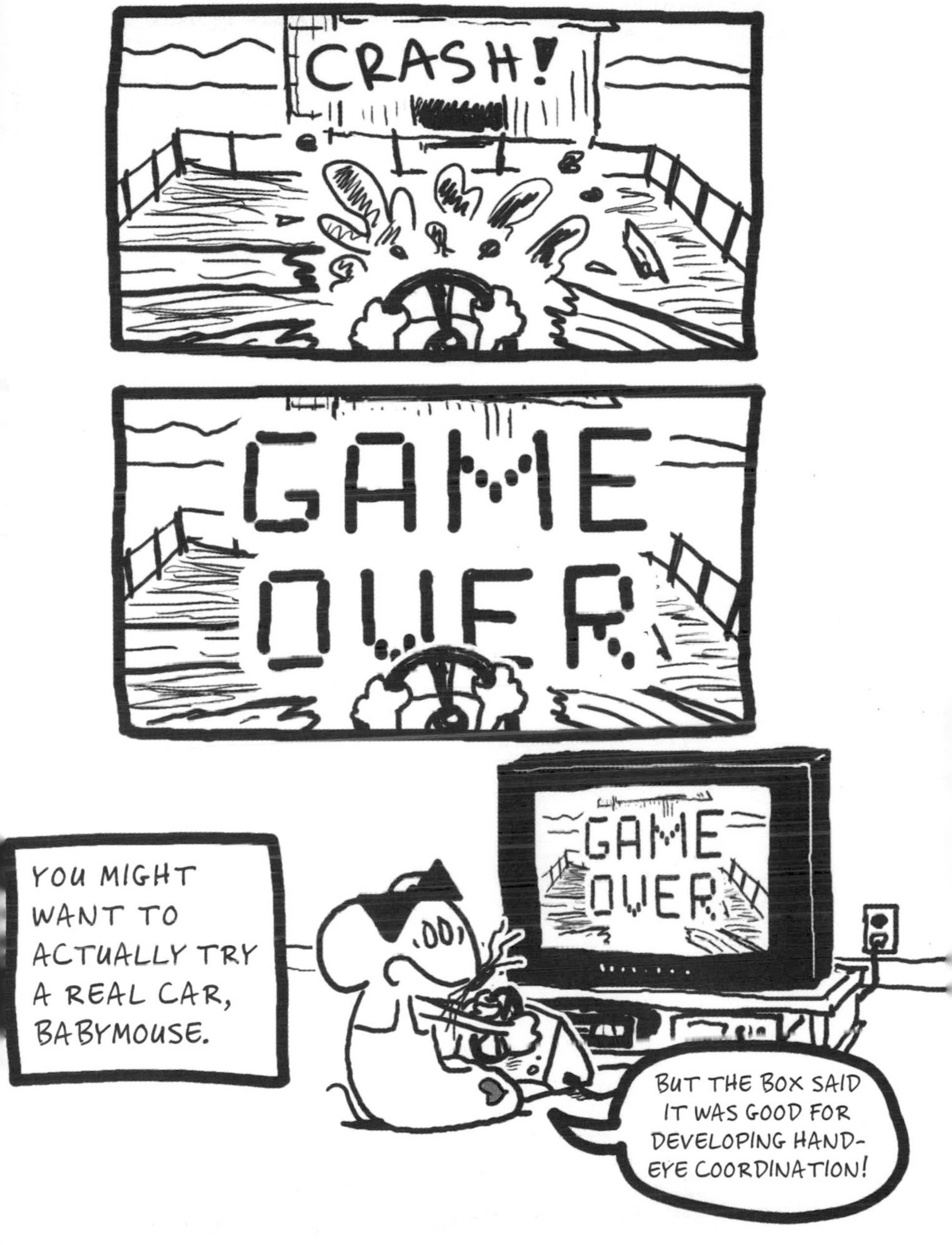
CRASH!
GAME OVER
GAME OVER
YOU MIGHT WANT TO ACTUALLY TRY A REAL CAR, BABYMOUSE.
BUT THE BOX SAID IT WAS GOOD FOR DEVELOPING HAND-EYE COORDINATION!

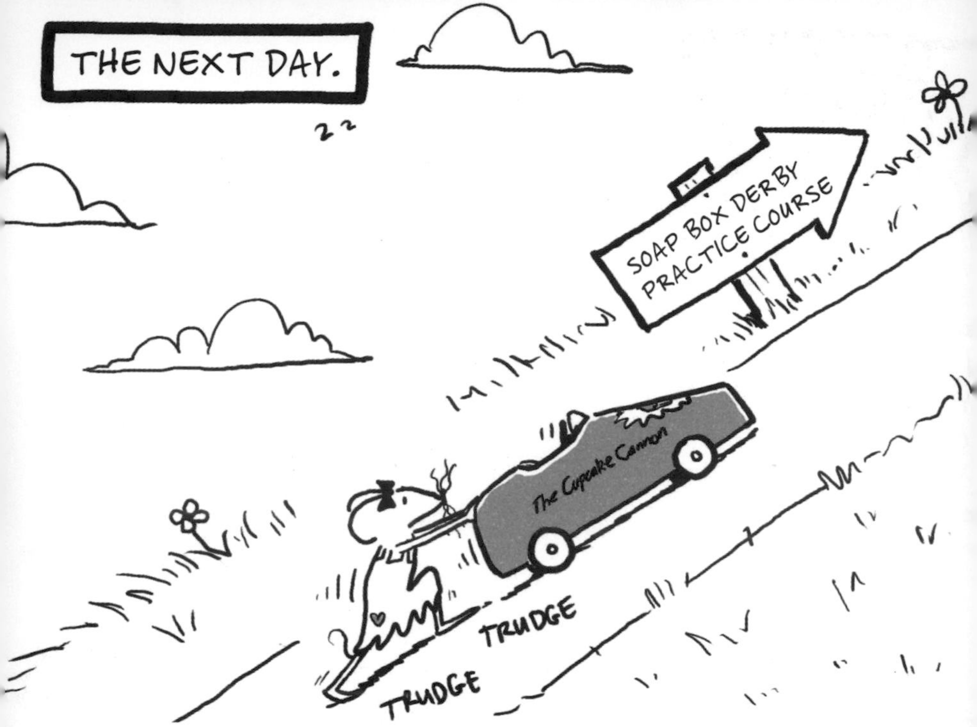
THE NEXT DAY.
z z
SOAP BOX DERBY
PRACTICE COURSE
The Cupcake Cannon
TRUDGE
TRUDGE

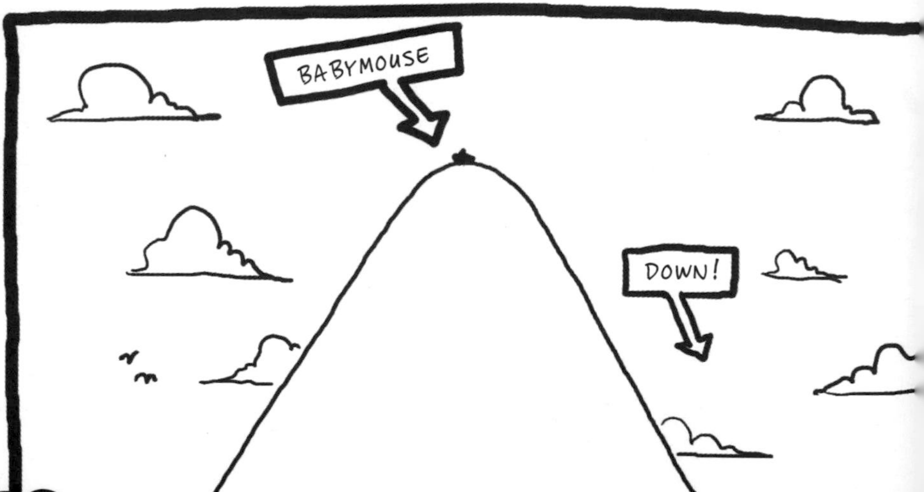
BABYMOUSE
DOWN!

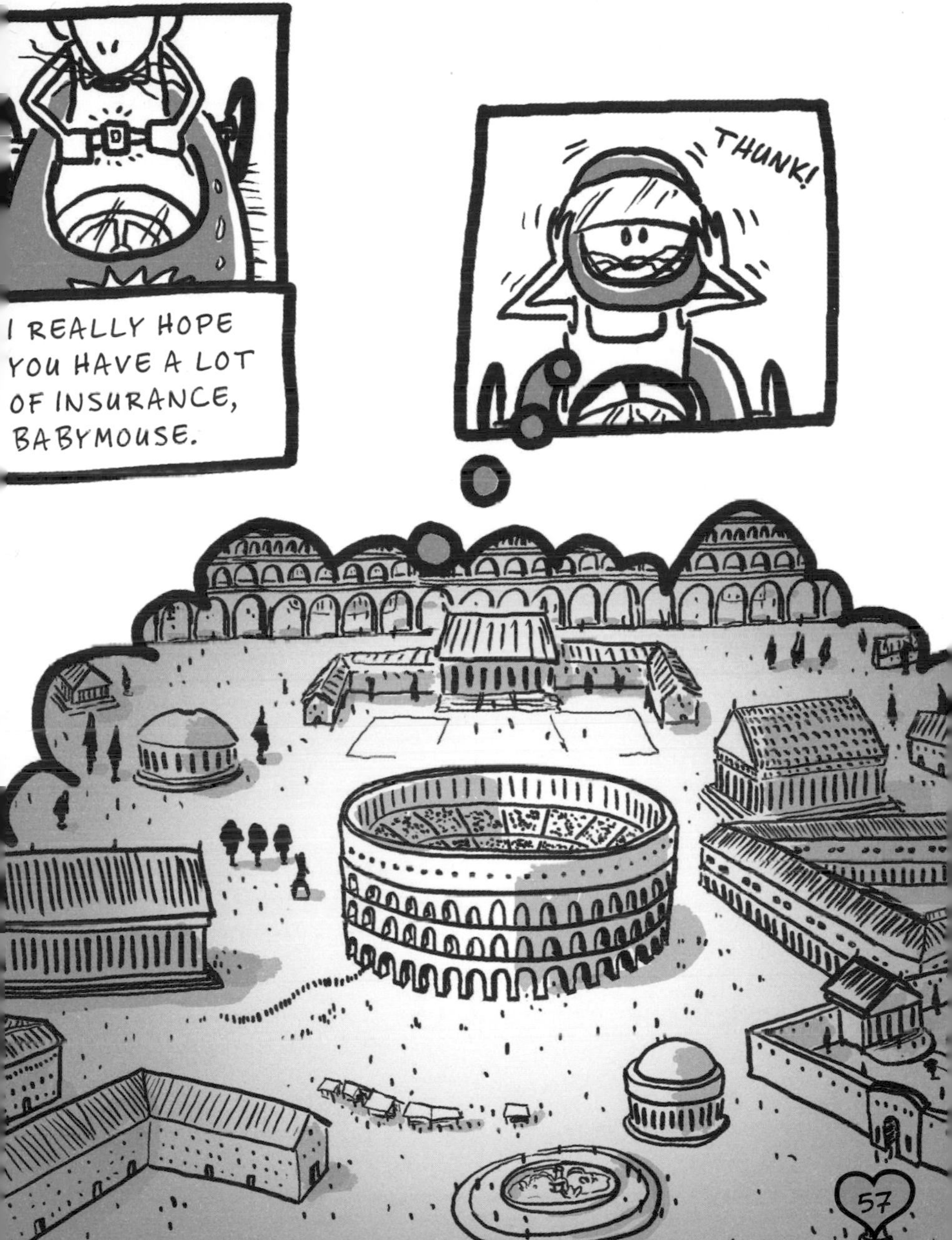
I REALLY HOPE YOU HAVE A LOT OF INSURANCE, BABYMOUSE.
THUNK!
D

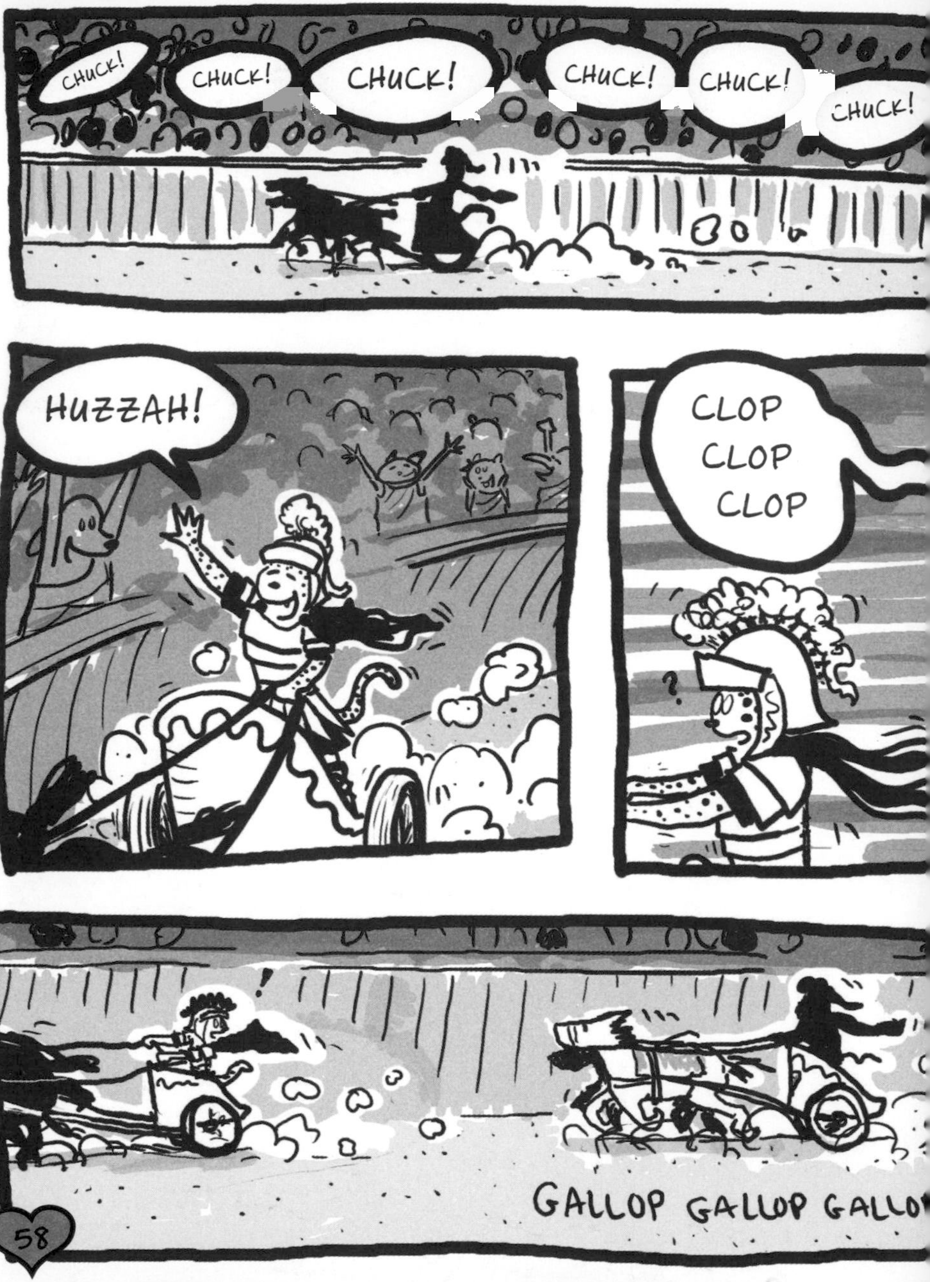
CHUCK!
CHUCK!
CHUCK!
CHUCK!
CHUCK!
CHUCK!
HUZZAH!
CLOP CLOP CLOP
GALLOP GALLOP GALLO

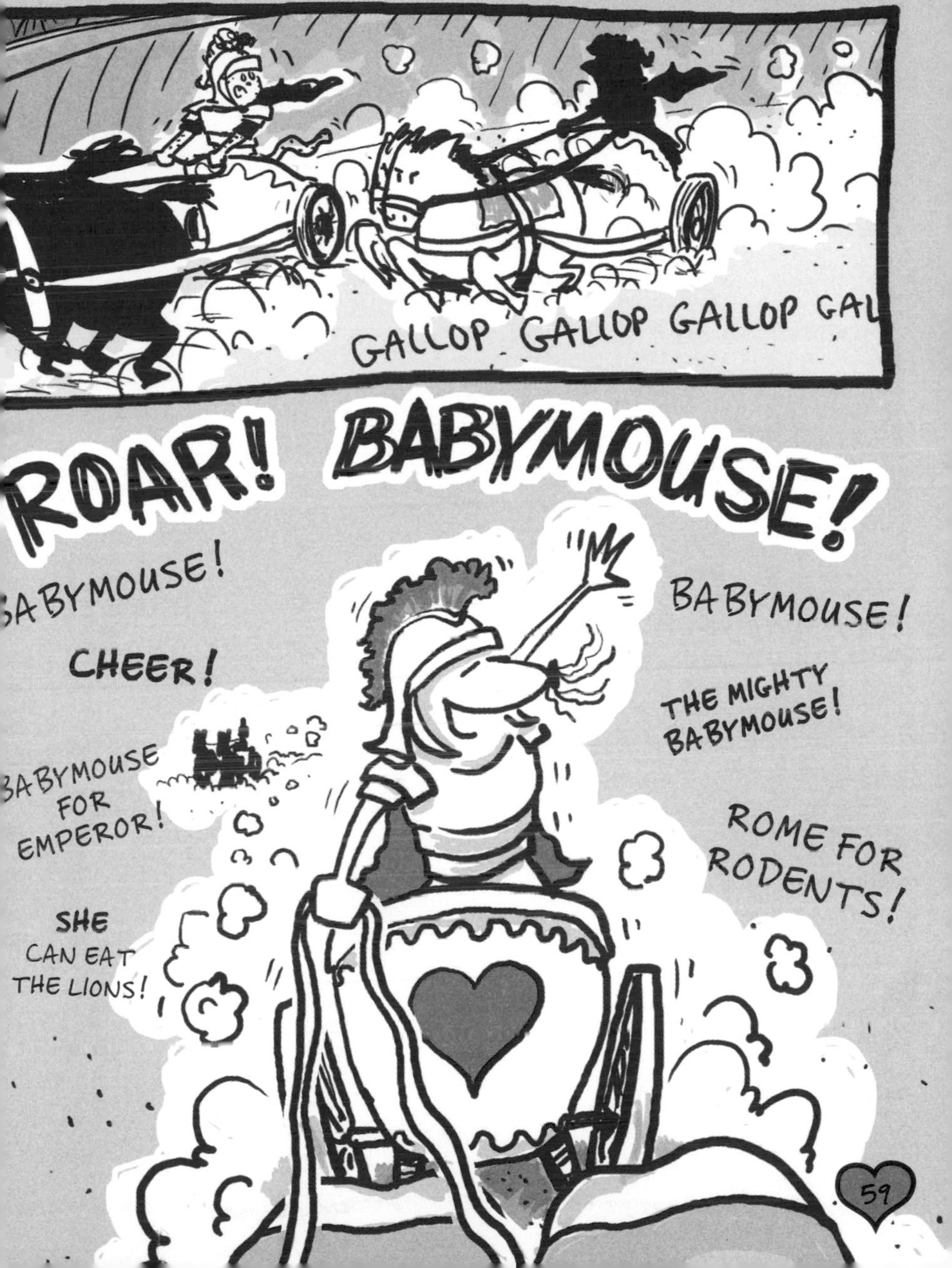
GALLOP GALLOP GALLOP GAL
ROAR! BABYMOUSE!
BABYMOUSE!
CHEER!
BABYMOUSE FOR EMPEROR!
SHE CAN EAT THE LIONS!
BABYMOUSE!
THE MIGHTY BABYMOUSE!
ROME FOR RODENTS!

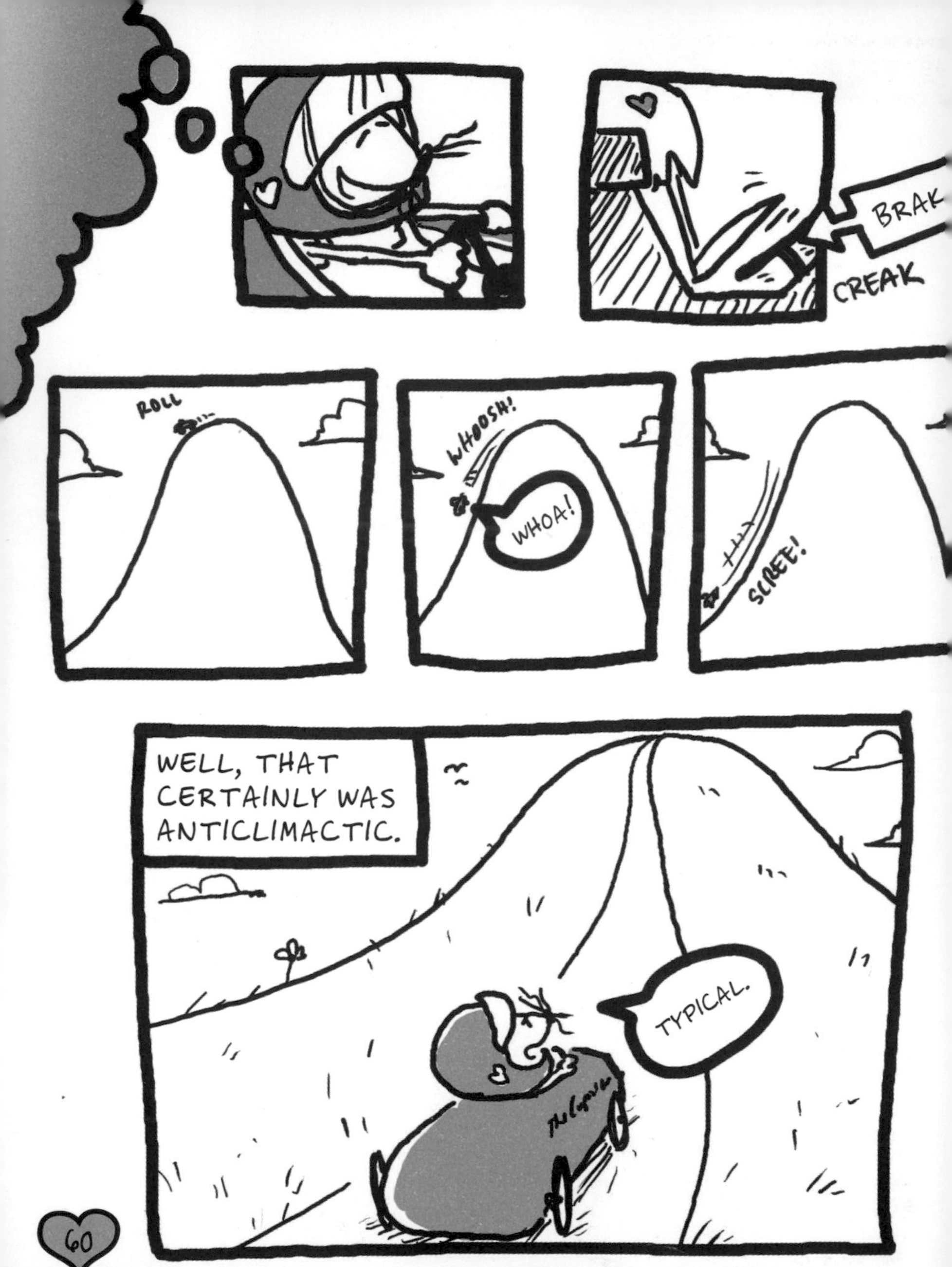
BRAK
CREAK
ROLL
WHOOSH!
WHOA!
SCREE!
WELL, THAT CERTAINLY WAS ANTICLIMACTIC.
TYPICAL.

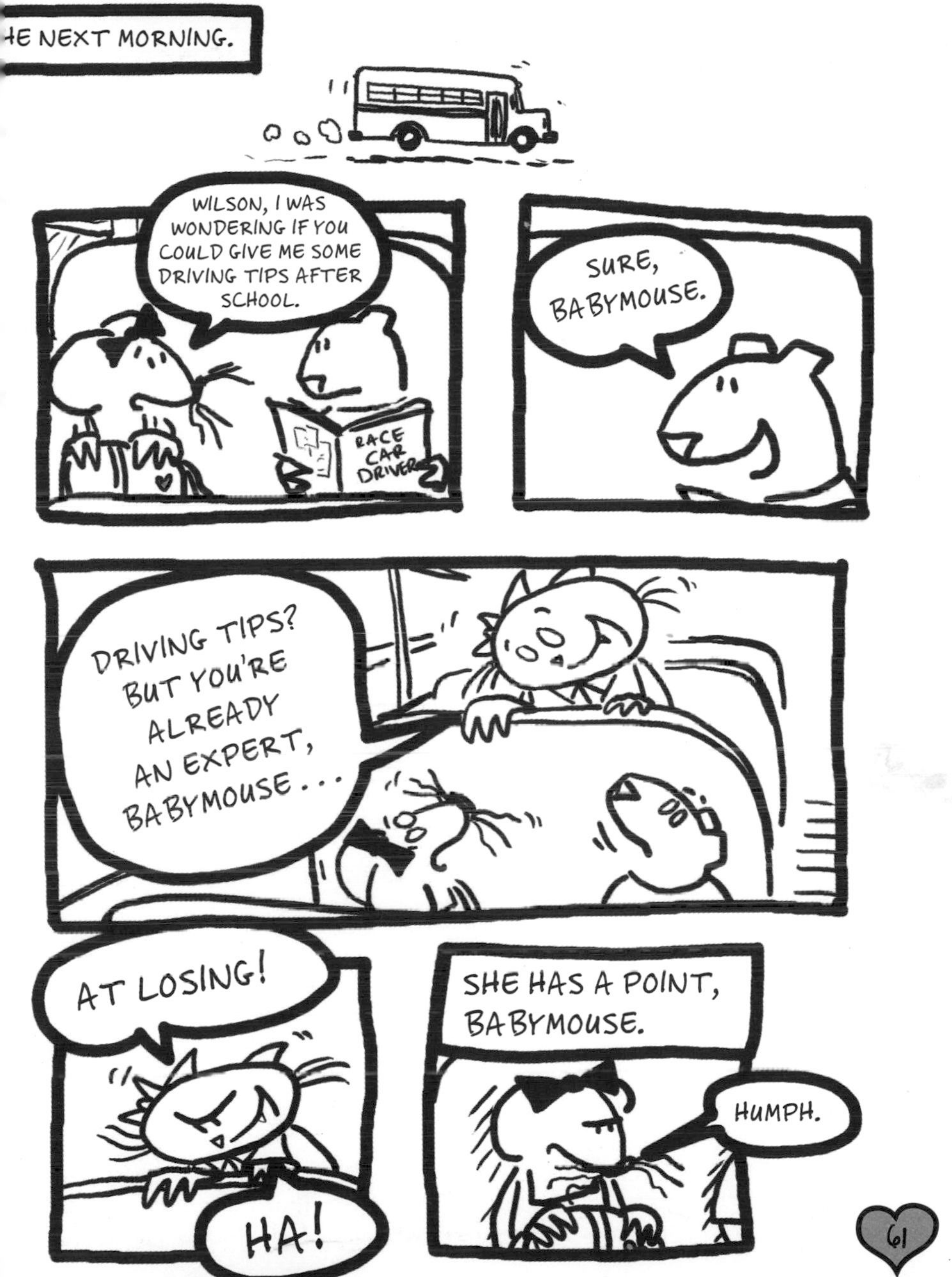
HE NEXT MORNING.
WILSON, I WAS WONDERING IF YOU COULD GIVE ME SOME DRIVING TIPS AFTER SCHOOL.
RACE CAR DRIVER
SURE, BABYMOUSE.
DRIVING TIPS? BUT YOU'RE ALREADY AN EXPERT, BABYMOUSE . . .
AT LOSING!
HA!
SHE HAS A POINT, BABYMOUSE.
HUMPH.

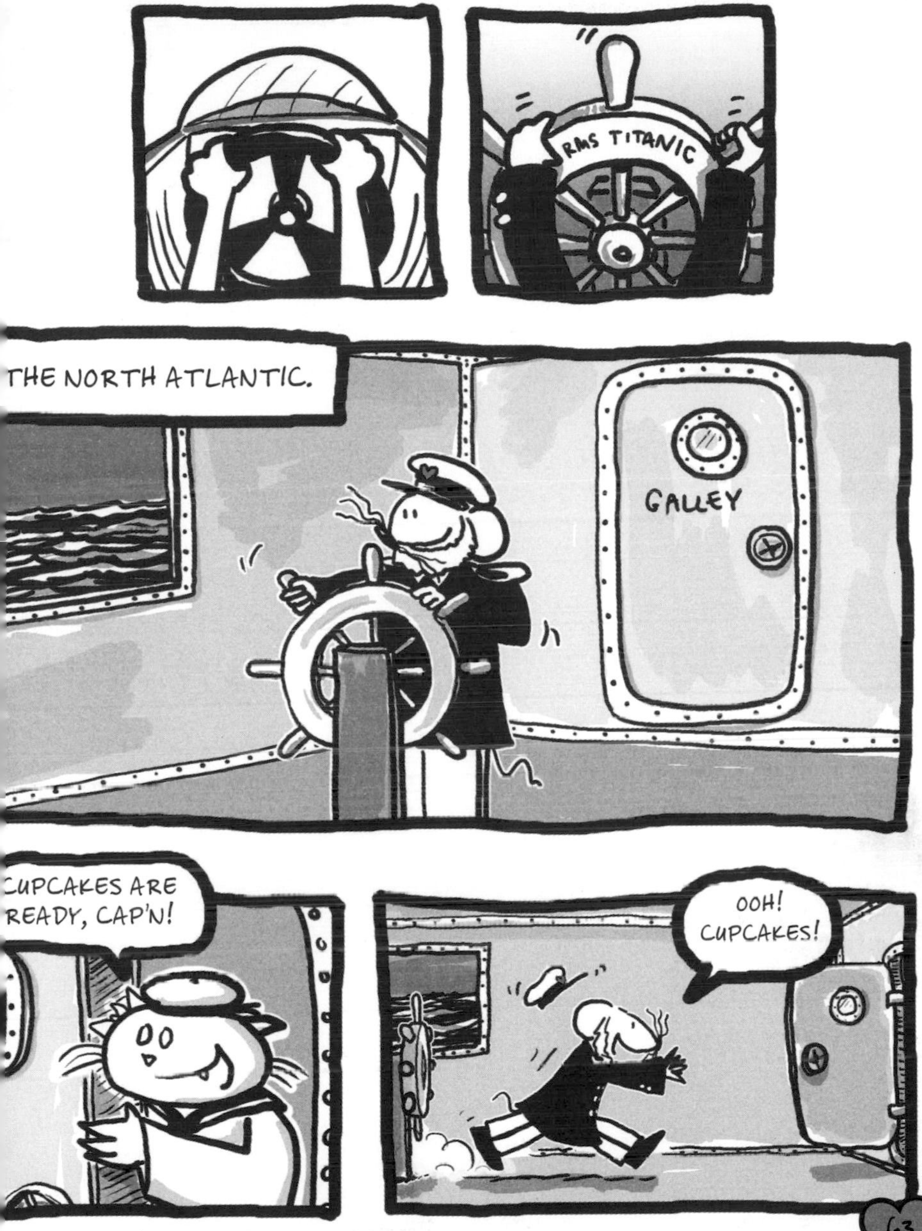
RMS TITANIC
THE NORTH ATLANTIC.
GALLEY
CUPCAKES ARE READY, CAP'N!
OOH! CUPCAKES!

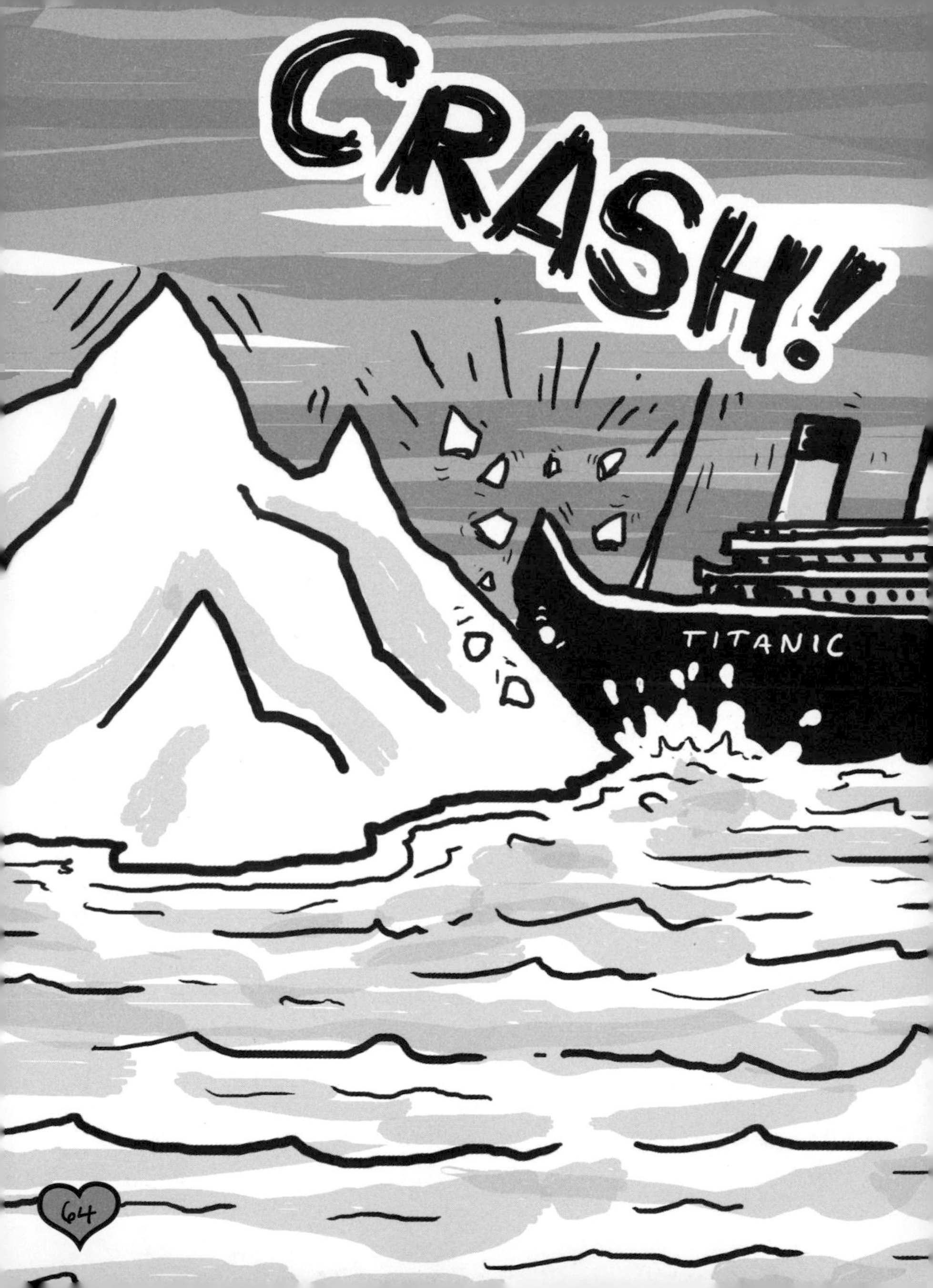
CRASH!
TITANIC

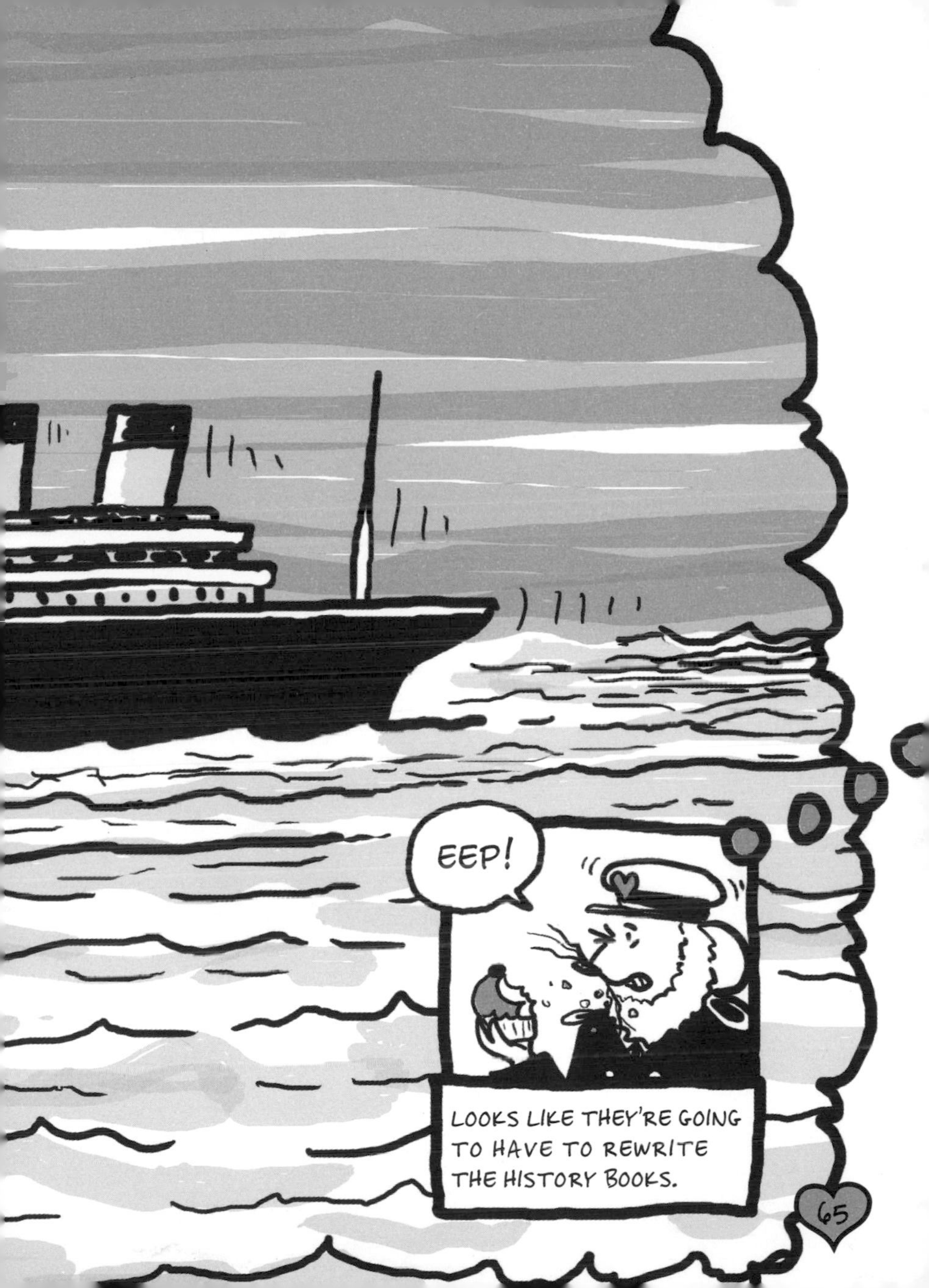
EEP!
LOOKS LIKE THEY'RE GOING TO HAVE TO REWRITE THE HISTORY BOOKS.

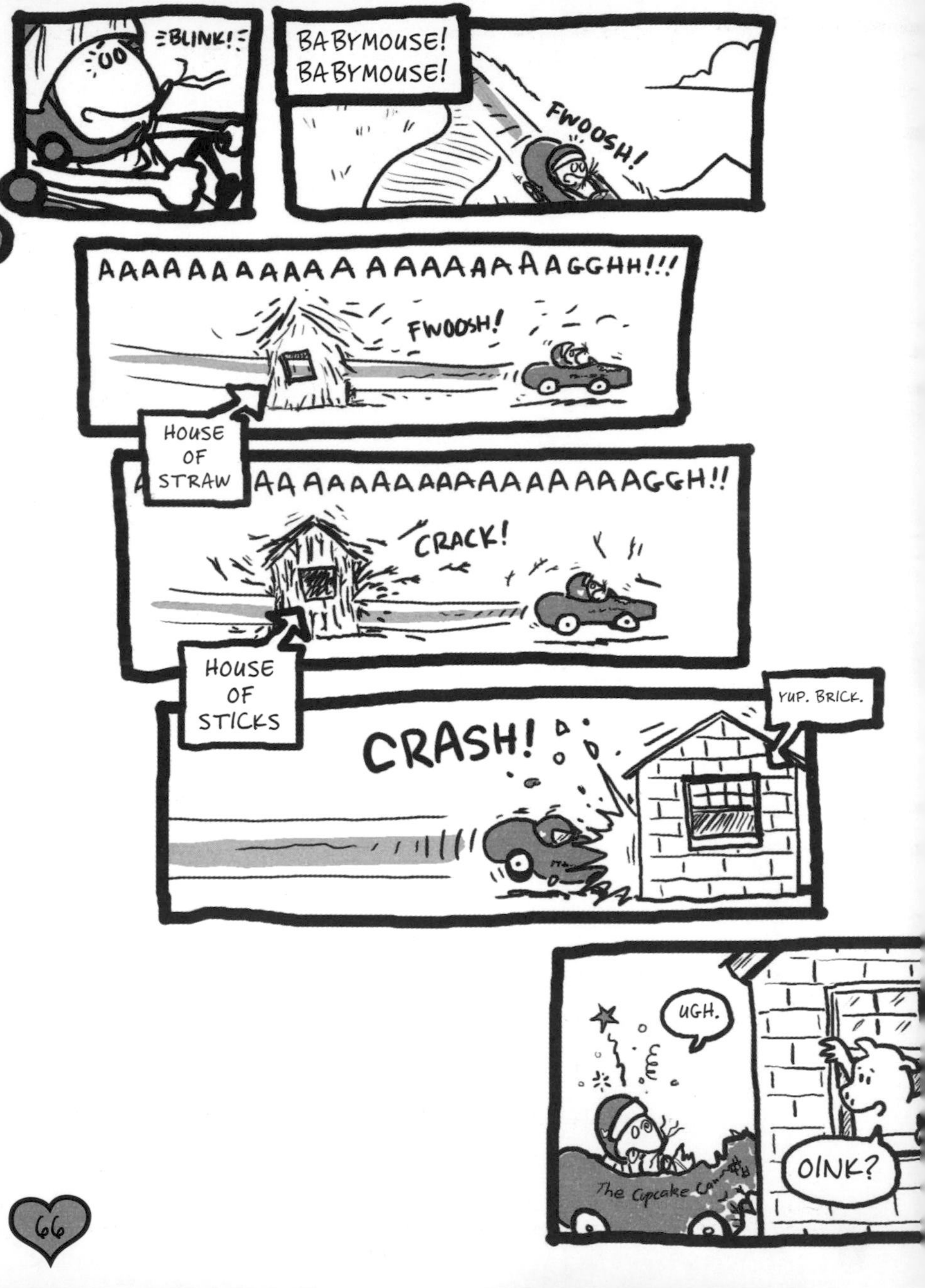
BLINK!
BABYMOUSE! BABYMOUSE!
FWOOSH!
AAAAAAAAAAA AAAAAAAAGGHH!!!
FWOOSH!
HOUSE OF STRAW
AAAAAAAAAAAAAAAAAAAAGGH!!
CRACK!
HOUSE OF STICKS
CRASH!
YUP. BRICK.
UGH.
OINK?

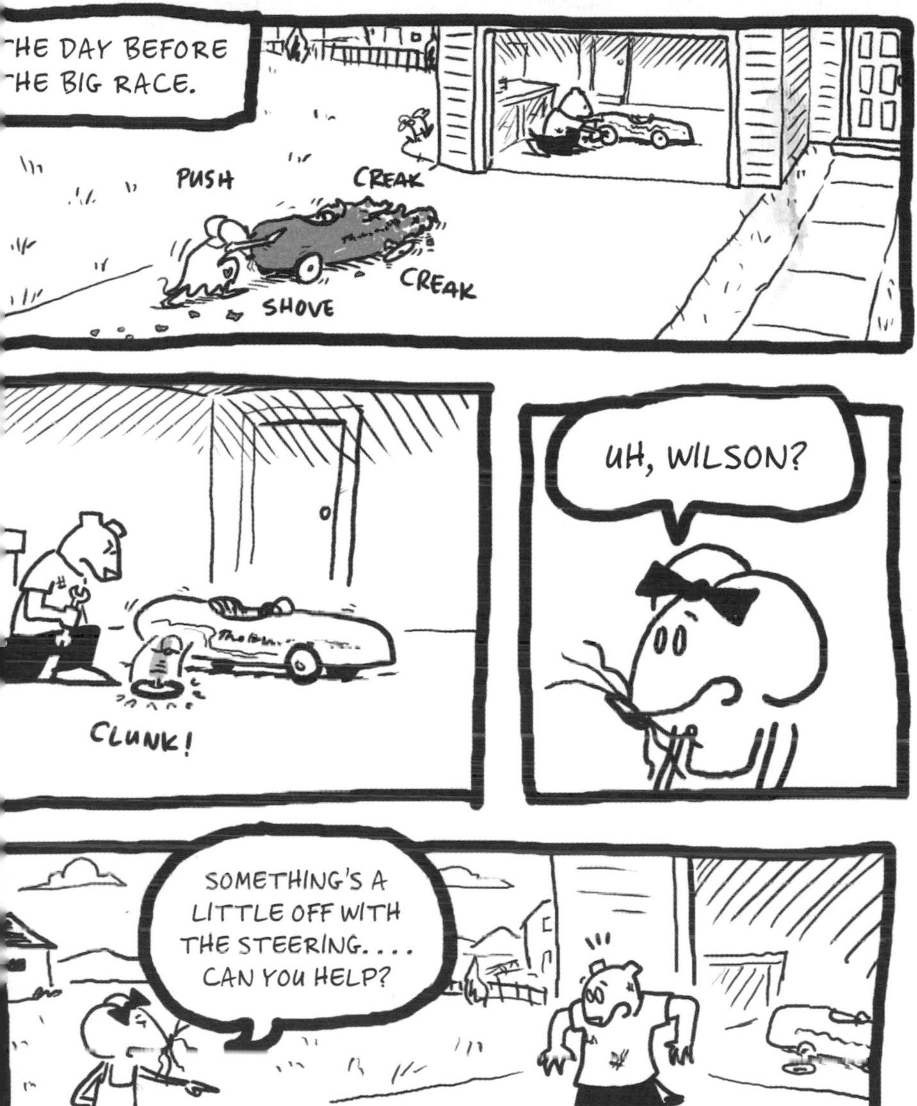
THE DAY BEFORE THE BIG RACE.
PUSH
CREAK
CREAK
SHOVE
CLUNK!
UH, WILSON?
SOMETHING'S A LITTLE OFF WITH THE STEERING. . . . CAN YOU HELP?
The Cupcake

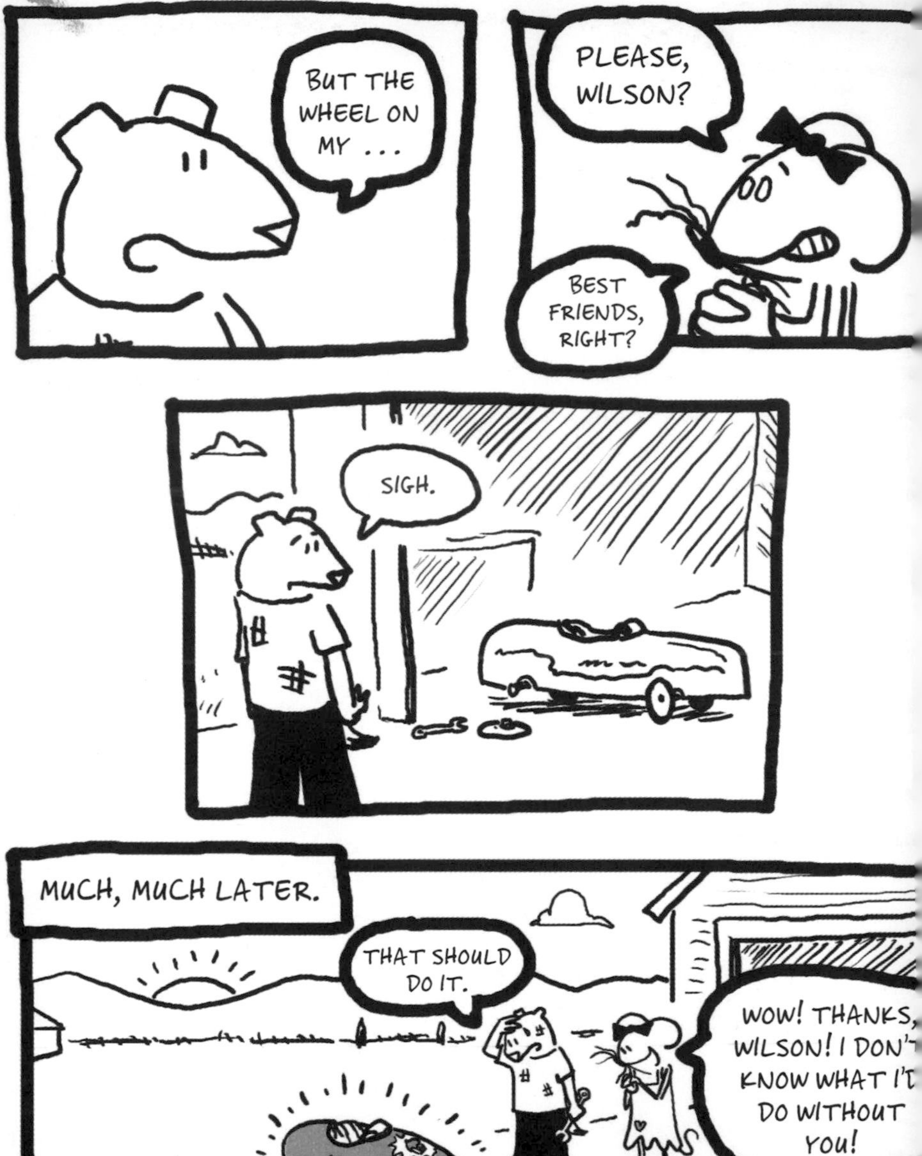
BUT THE WHEEL ON MY . . .
PLEASE, WILSON?
BEST FRIENDS, RIGHT?
SIGH.
MUCH, MUCH LATER.
THAT SHOULD DO IT.
WOW! THANKS, WILSON! I DON'T KNOW WHAT I'D DO WITHOUT YOU!

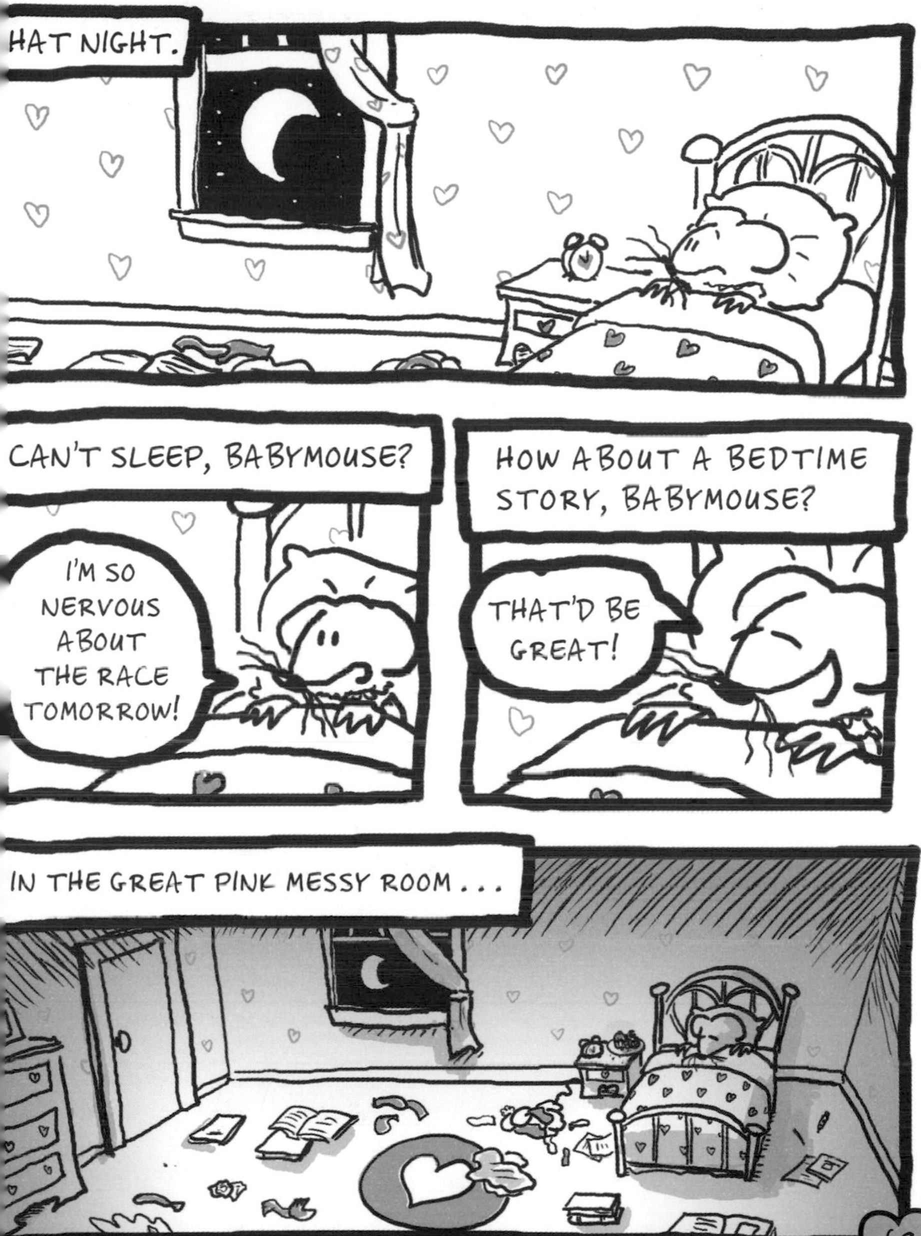
HAT NIGHT.
CAN'T SLEEP, BABYMOUSE?
I'M SO NERVOUS ABOUT THE RACE TOMORROW!
HOW ABOUT A BEDTIME STORY, BABYMOUSE?
THAT'D BE GREAT!
IN THE GREAT PINK MESSY ROOM . . .

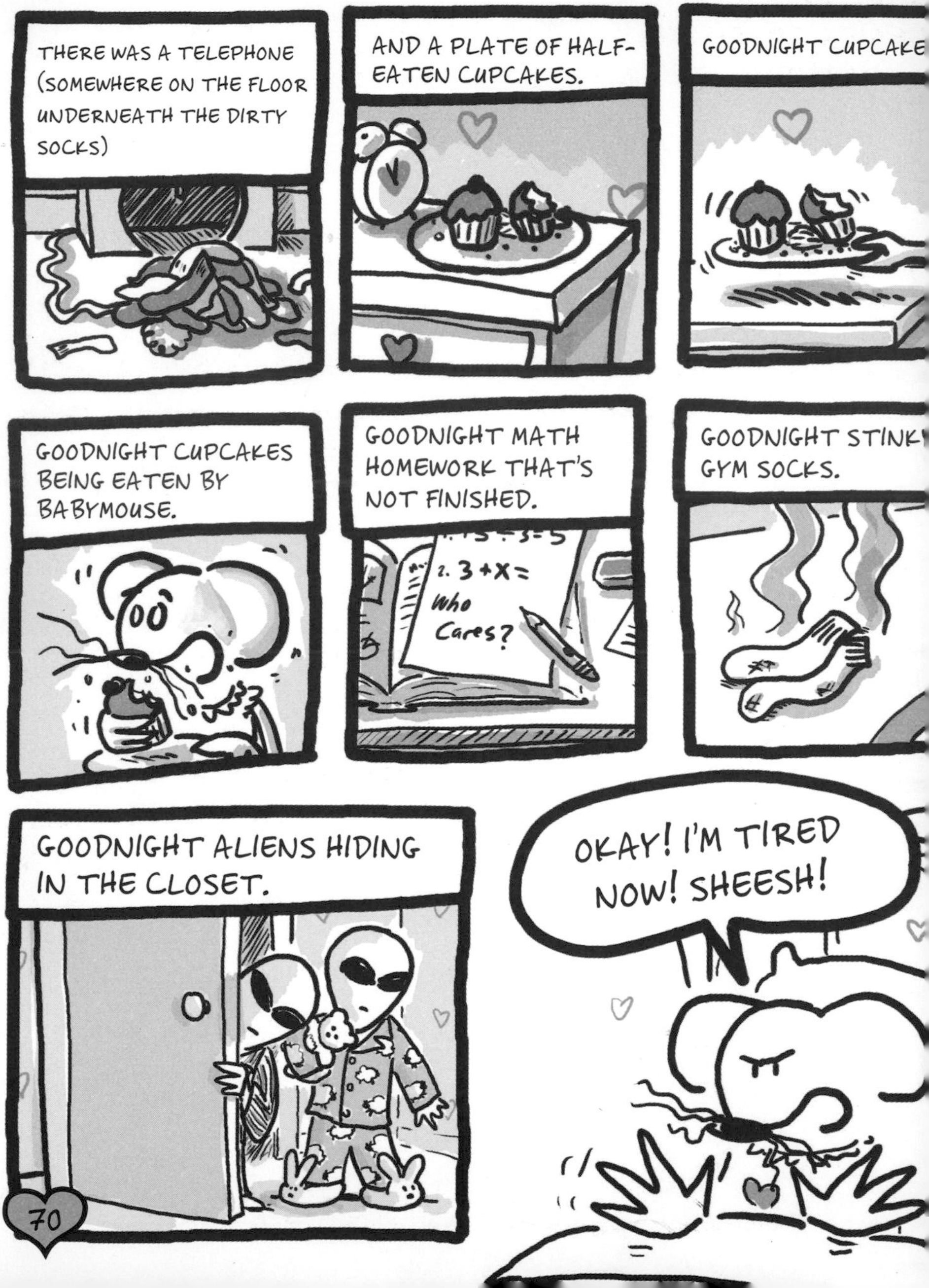
THERE WAS A TELEPHONE (SOMEWHERE ON THE FLOOR UNDERNEATH THE DIRTY SOCKS)
AND A PLATE OF HALF-EATEN CUPCAKES.
GOODNIGHT CUPCAKE
GOODNIGHT CUPCAKES BEING EATEN BY BABYMOUSE.
GOODNIGHT MATH HOMEWORK THAT'S NOT FINISHED.
2. 3 + X =
Who Cares?
GOODNIGHT STINK
GYM SOCKS.
GOODNIGHT ALIENS HIDING IN THE CLOSET.
OKAY! I'M TIRED NOW! SHEESH!

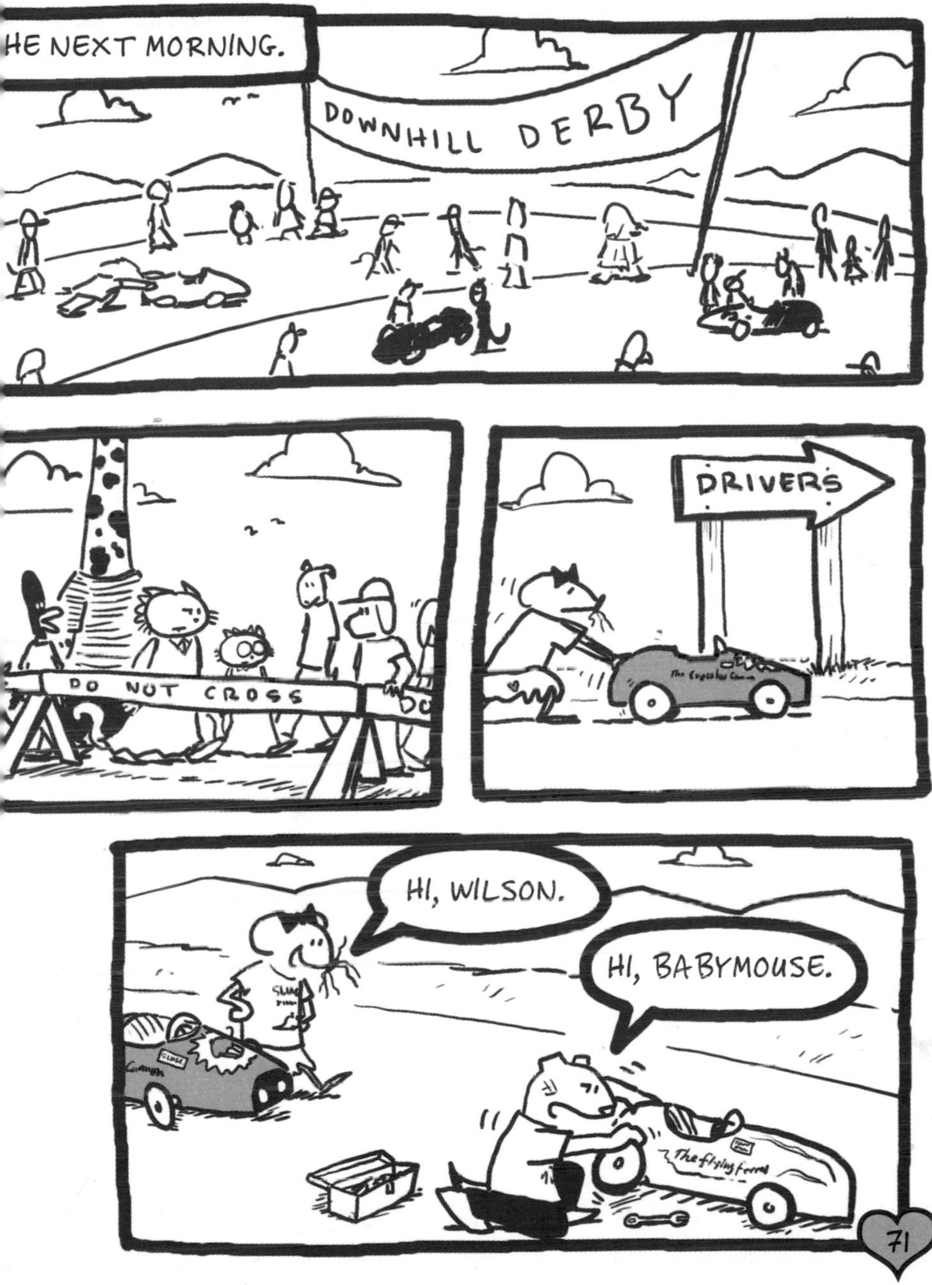
HE NEXT MORNING.
DOWNHILL DERBY
DO NOT CROSS
DRIVERS
HI, WILSON.
HI, BABYMOUSE.

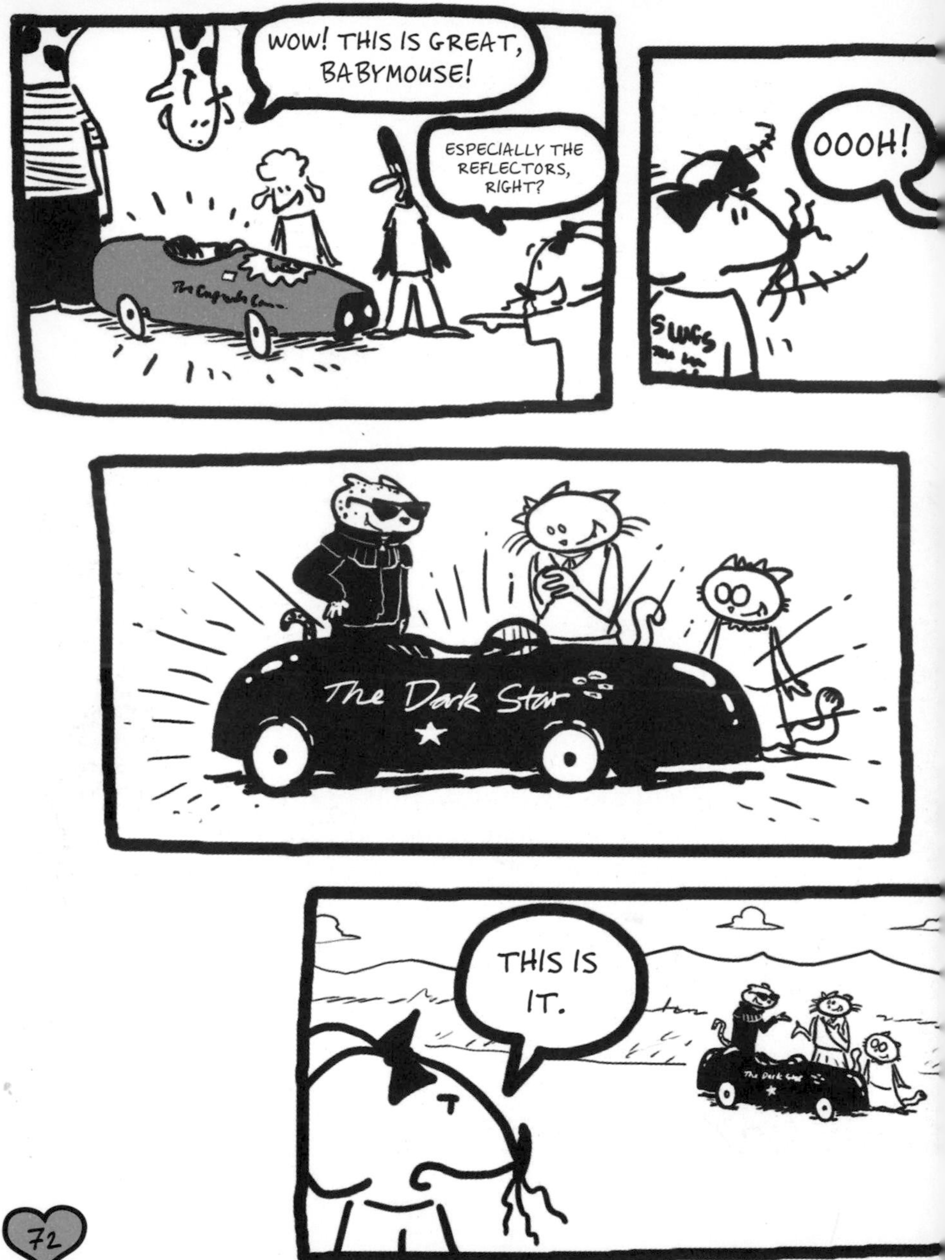
WOW! THIS IS GREAT, BABYMOUSE!
ESPECIALLY THE REFLECTORS, RIGHT?
OOOH!
SLUGS
The Dark Star
THIS IS IT.

SOAP BOX

CHAPTER VII
A NEW CUPCAKE

It is a dark time for the
REBELLION. The brave pilot,
BABYMOUSE, has badgered her
best friend into building her a

SOAP BOX DERBY CAR.

SOAP BOX DERBY CAR.

Little does she know that the villainous CHUCK E. CHEETAH is going to totally mop the floor with her, since he has actually practiced every day for years and she can't avoid crashing into pigpens.

into pigpens.

Now the hour has come at last that will spell certain doom for the blah blah blah blah... are you still reading this?

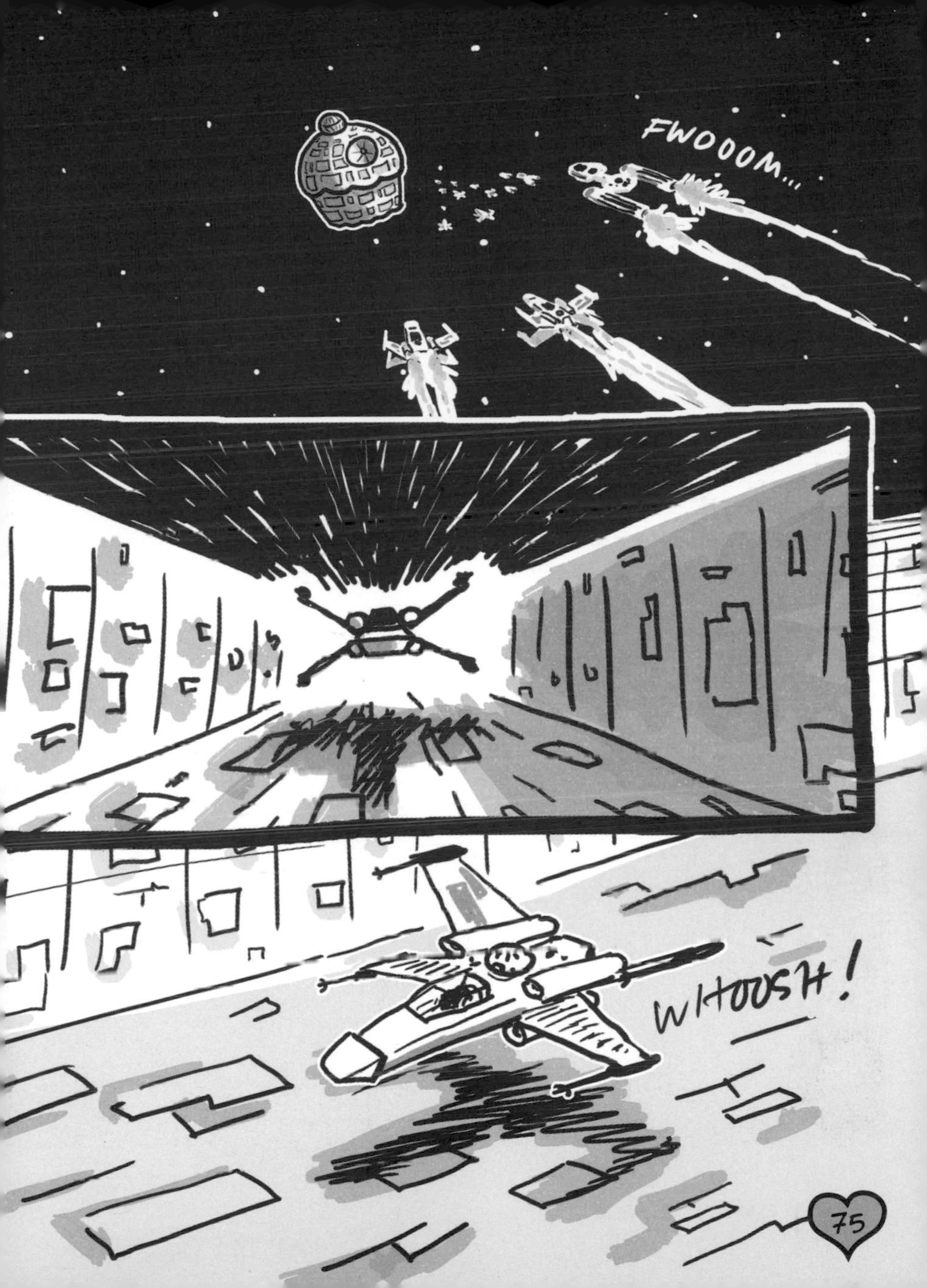
FWOOOM...
WHOOSH!

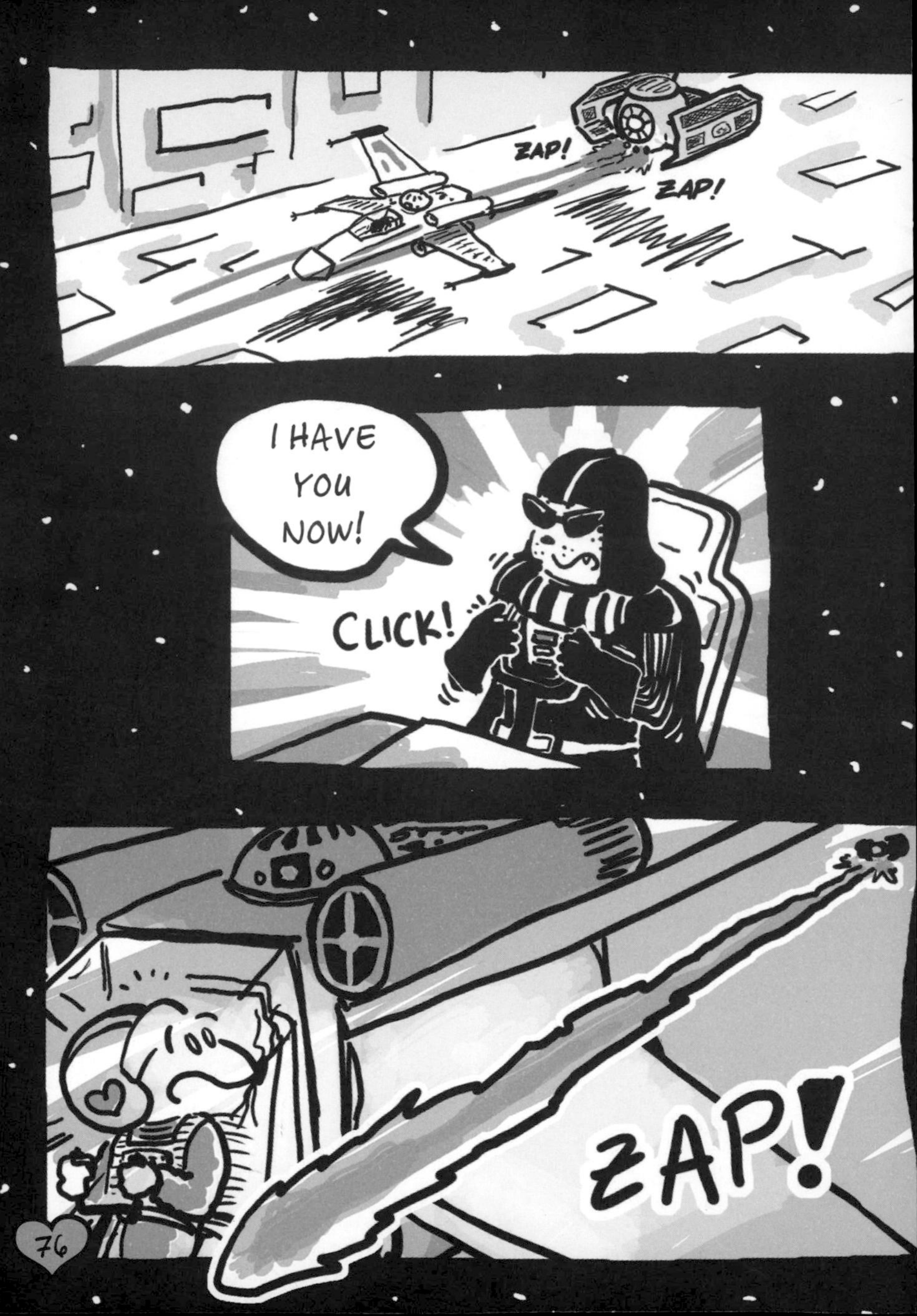
ZAP!
ZAP!
I HAVE YOU NOW!
CLICK!
ZAP!

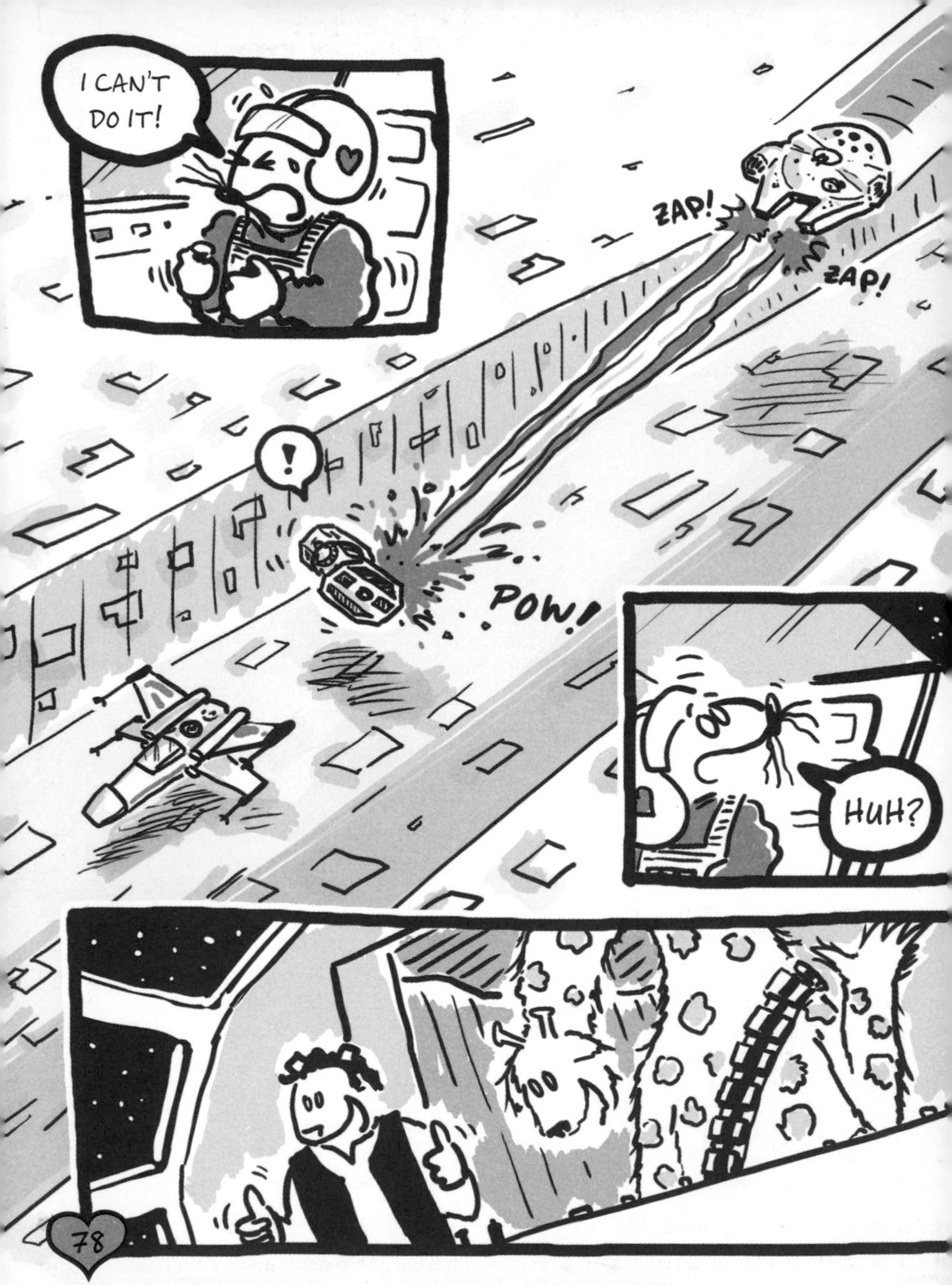
I CAN'T DO IT!
ZAP!
ZAP!
!
POW!
HUH?

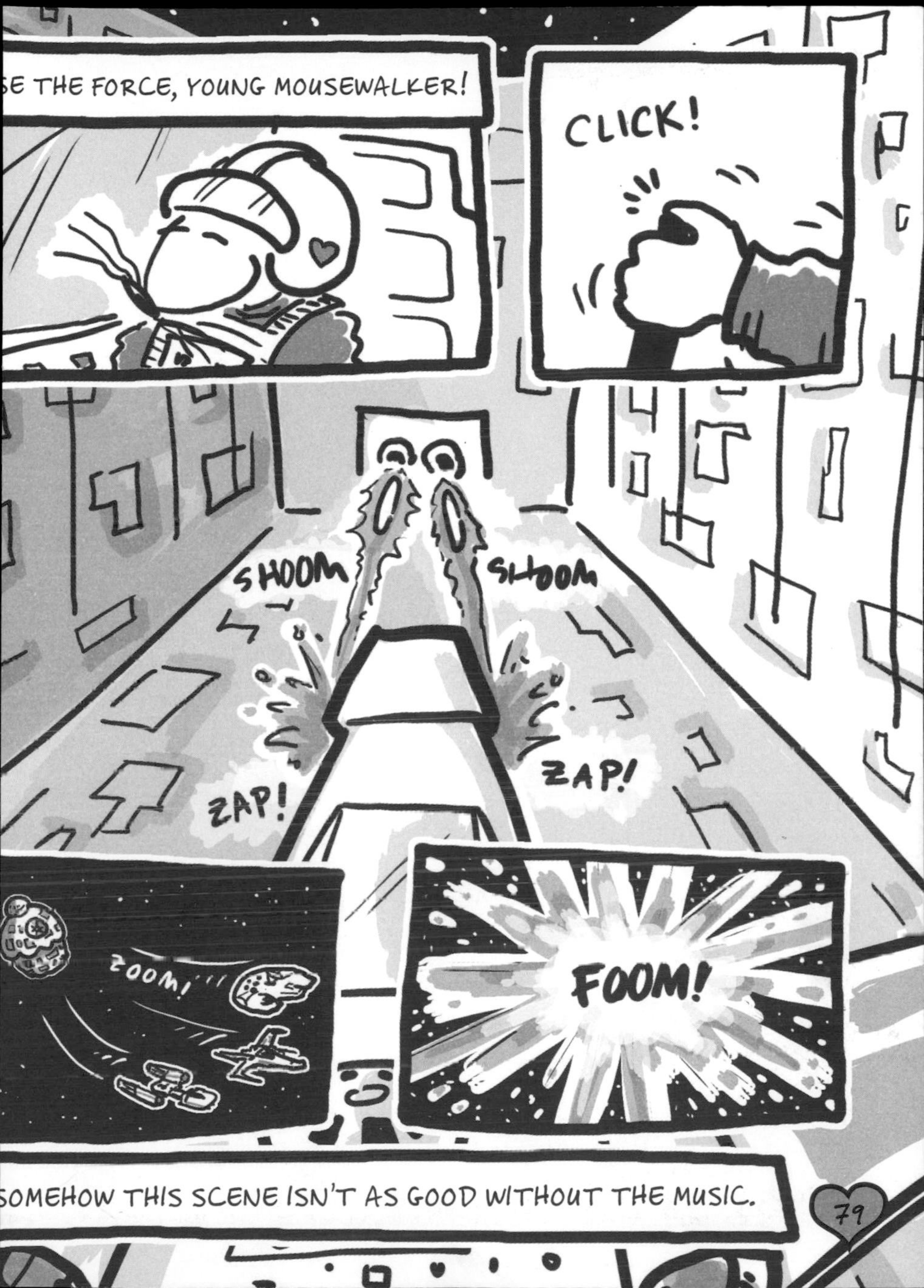
SE THE FORCE, YOUNG MOUSEWALKER!
CLICK!
SHOOM
SHOOM
ZAP!
ZAP!
ZOOM!
FOOM!
SOMEHOW THIS SCENE ISN'T AS GOOD WITHOUT THE MUSIC.

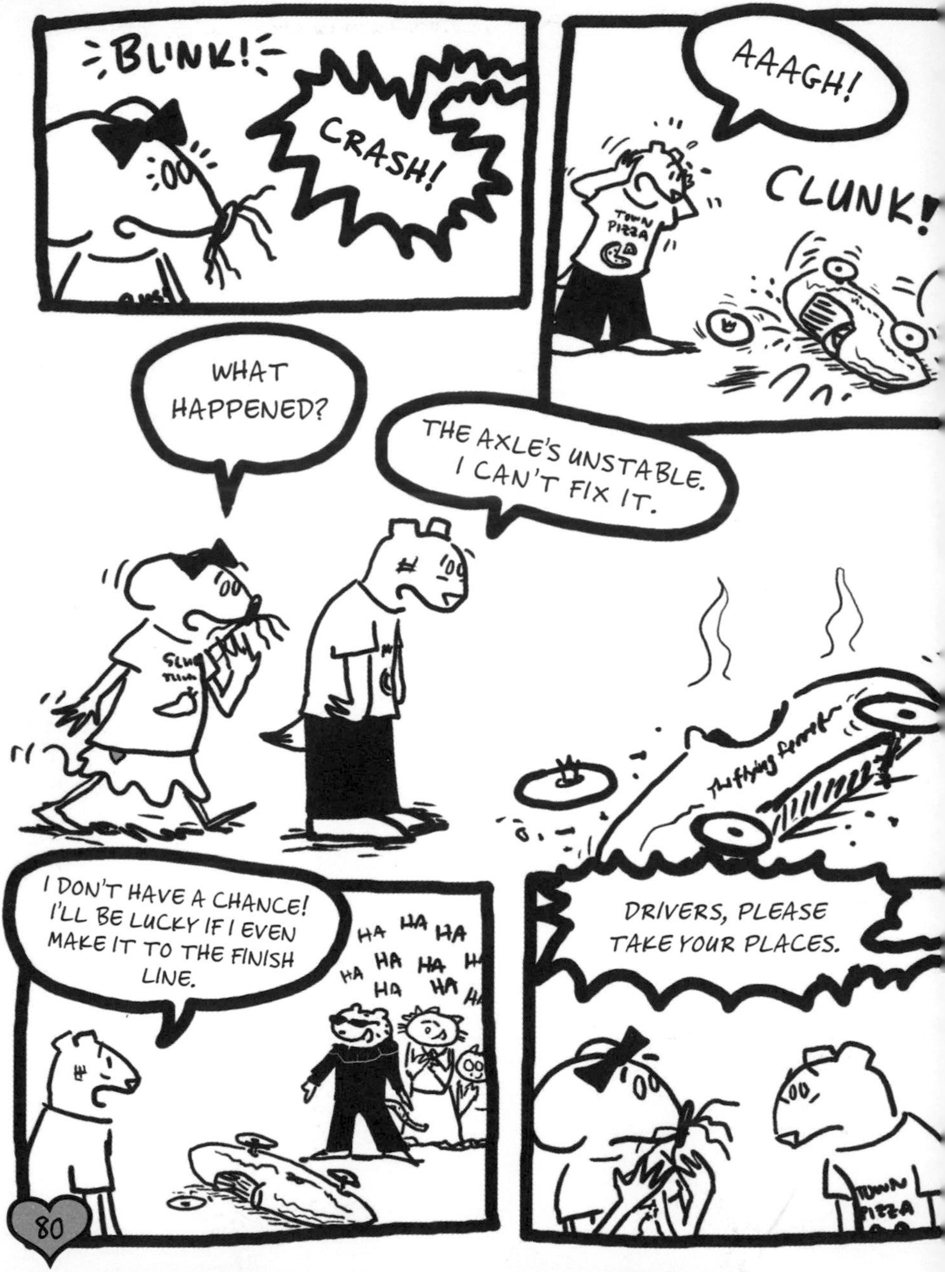
BLINK!
CRASH!
AAAGH!
CLUNK!
TOWN PIZZA
WHAT HAPPENED?
THE AXLE'S UNSTABLE. I CAN'T FIX IT.
The flying ferret
I DON'T HAVE A CHANCE! I'LL BE LUCKY IF I EVEN MAKE IT TO THE FINISH LINE.
HA HA HA HA HA HA HA HA
DRIVERS, PLEASE TAKE YOUR PLACES.
TOWN PIZZA

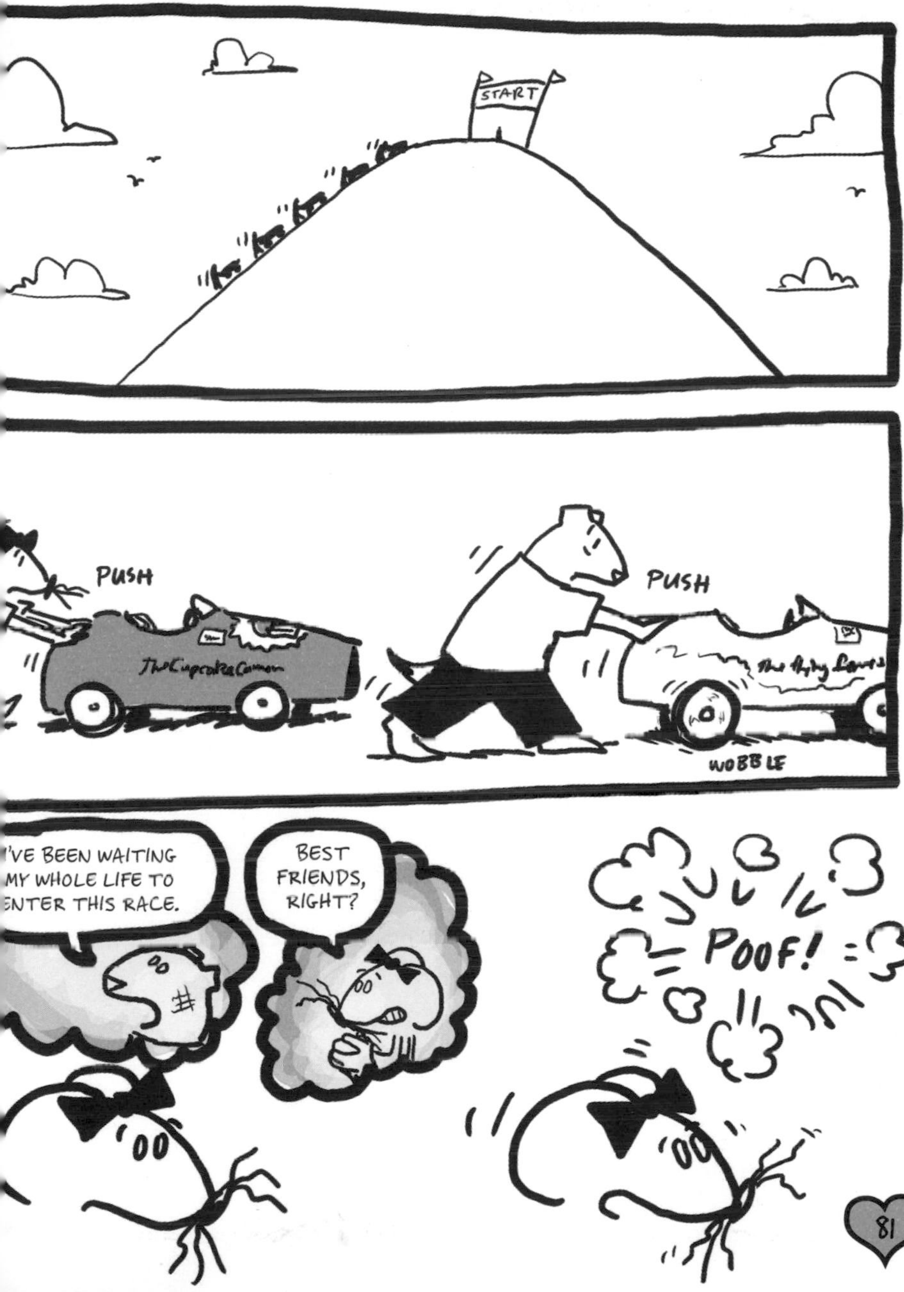
START
PUSH
PUSH
WOBBLE
I'VE BEEN WAITING MY WHOLE LIFE TO ENTER THIS RACE.
BEST FRIENDS, RIGHT?
POOF!

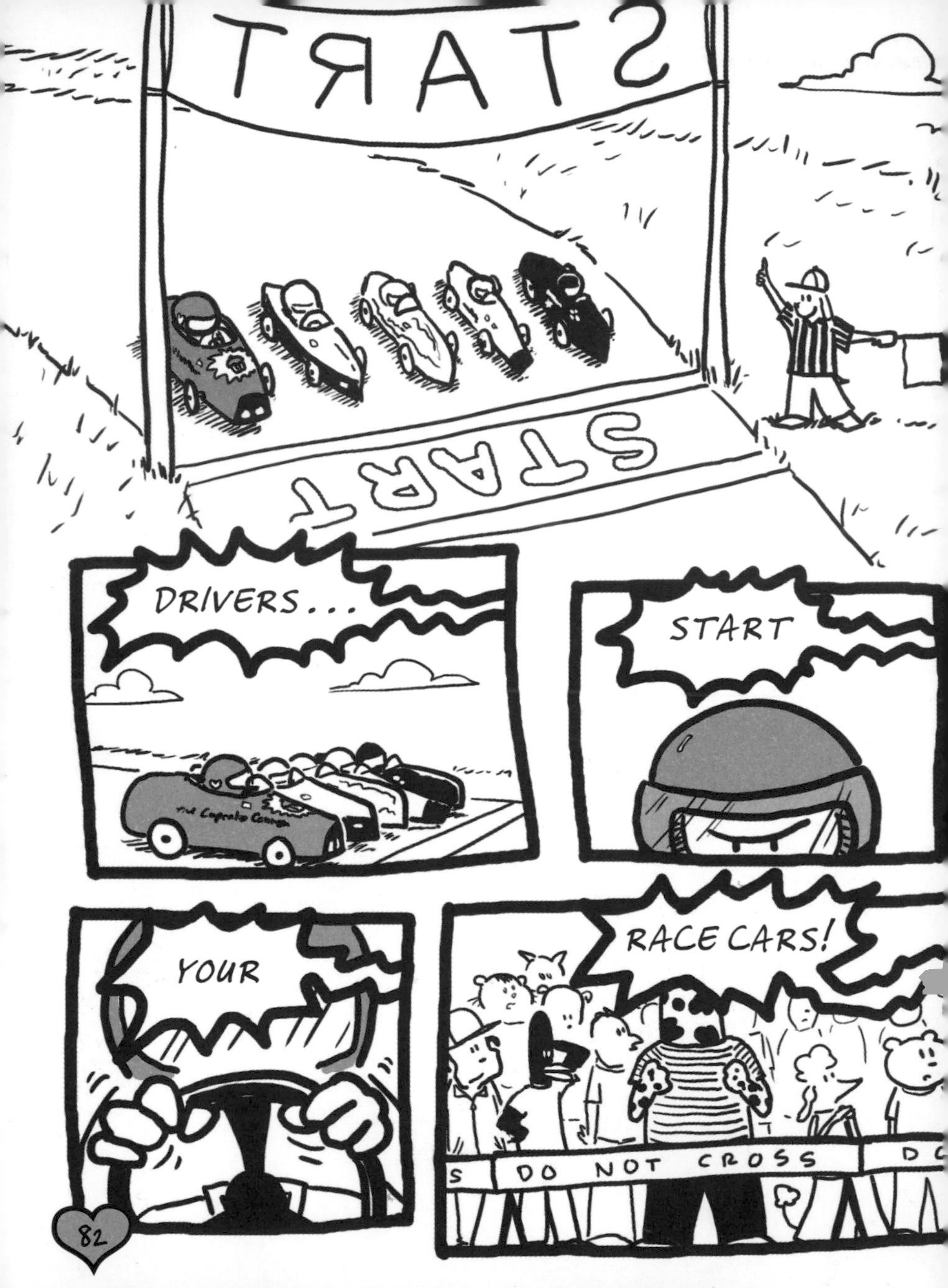
DRIVERS...
START
YOUR
RACE CARS!
DO NOT CROSS

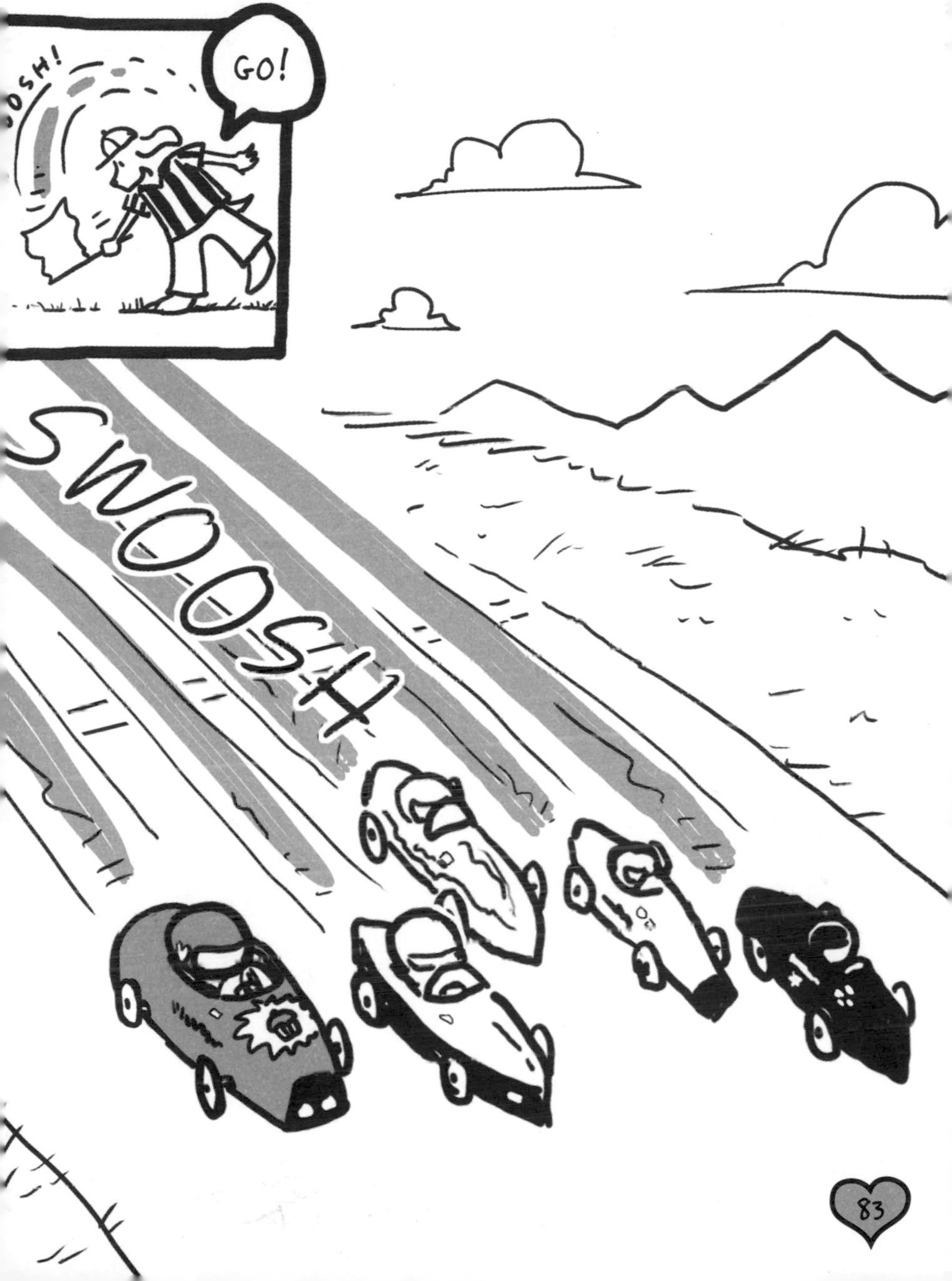
GO!
SWOOSH

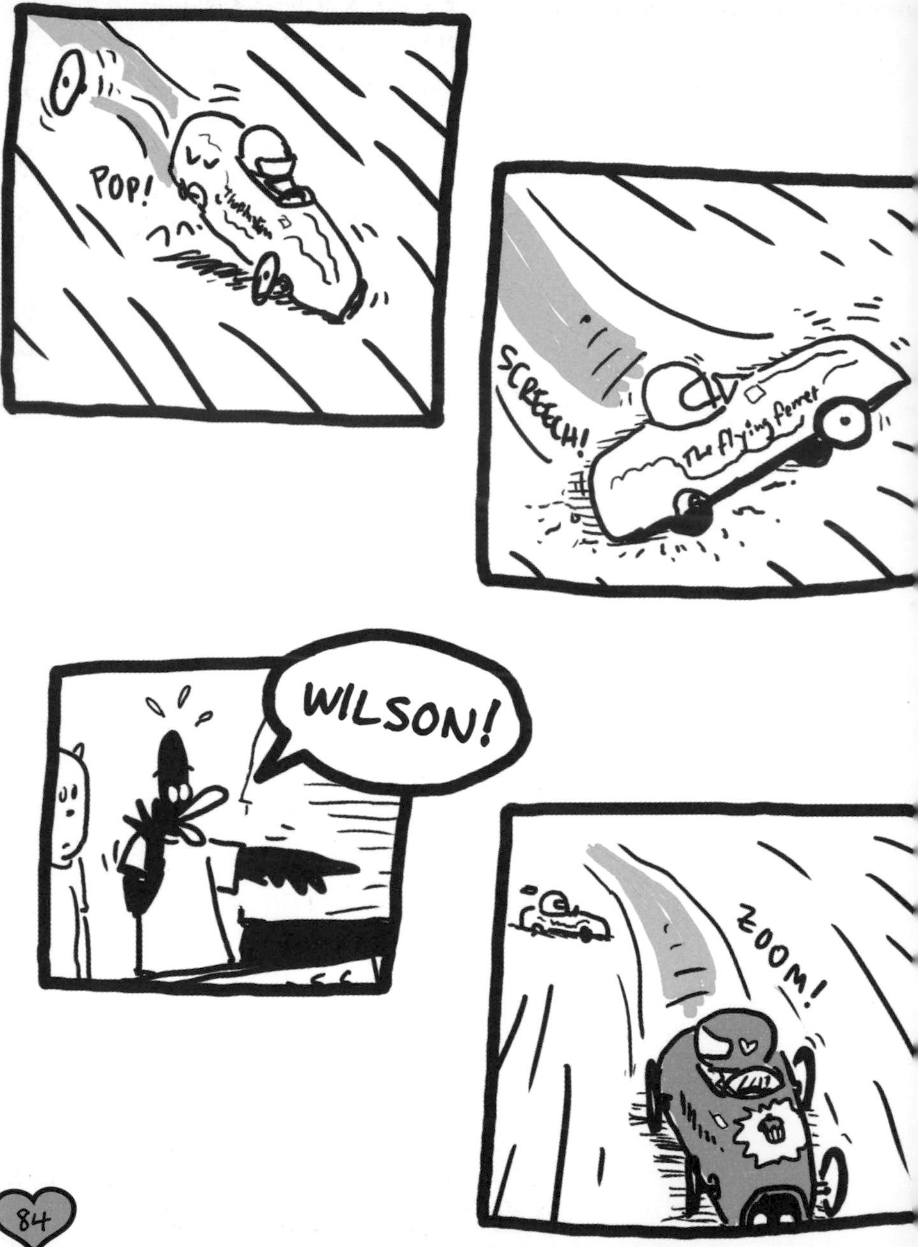
POP!
SCREECH!
The flying ferret
WILSON!
ZOOM!

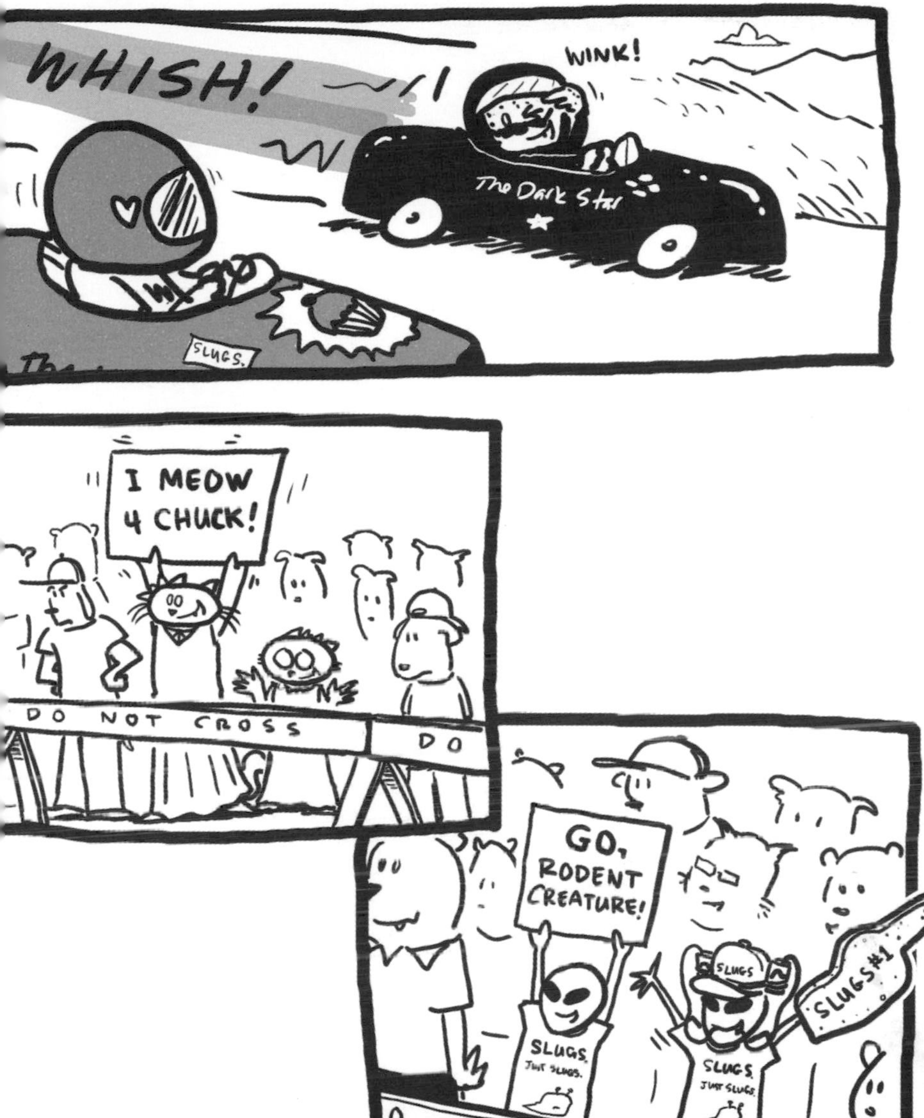
WHISH!
WINK!
The Dark Star
SLUGS.
I MEOW 4 CHUCK!
DO NOT CROSS
DO
GO, RODENT CREATURE!
SLUGS
SLUGS #1
SLUGS. JUST SLUGS.
SLUGS. JUST SLUGS.
O NOT CROSS

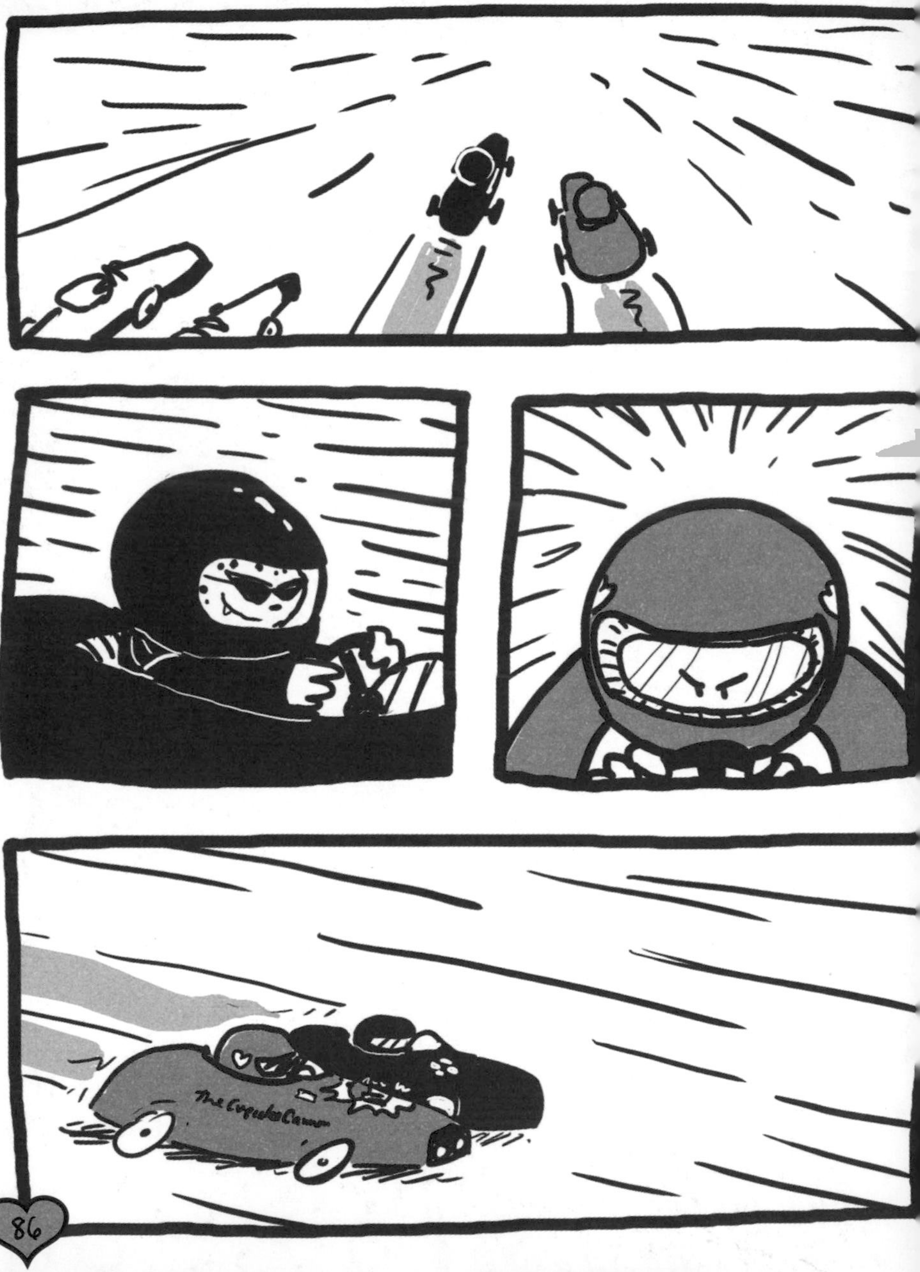

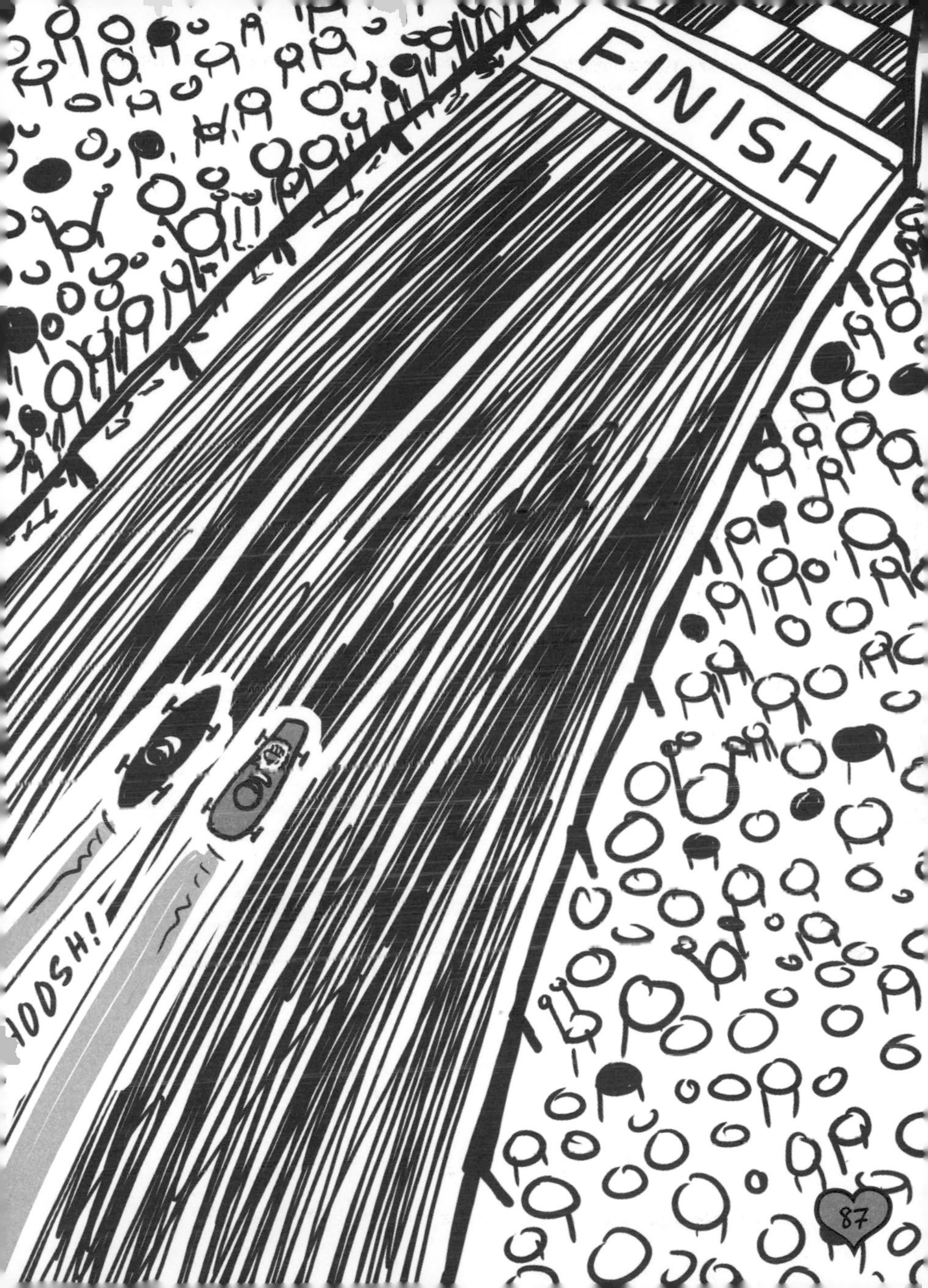
FINISH
HOOSH!

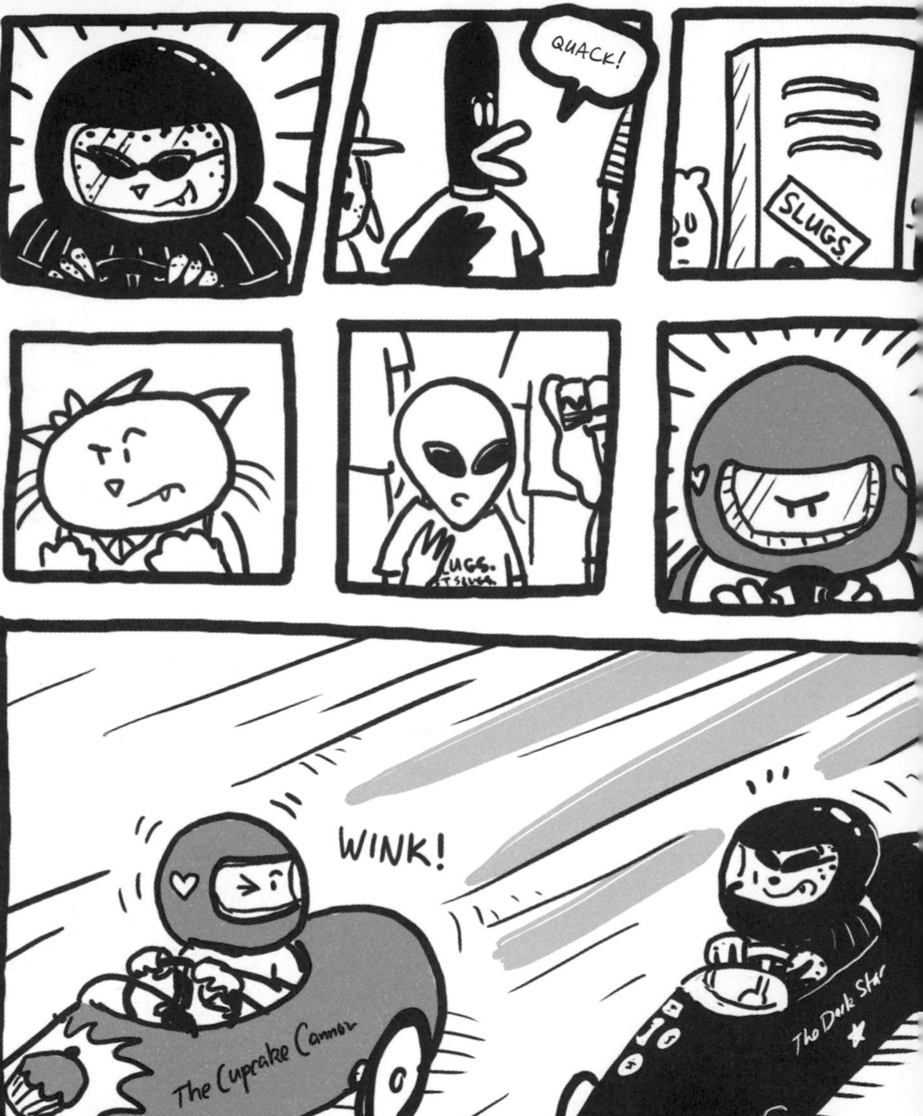
QUACK!
SLUGS
WINK!
The Cupcake Cannon
The Dark Star

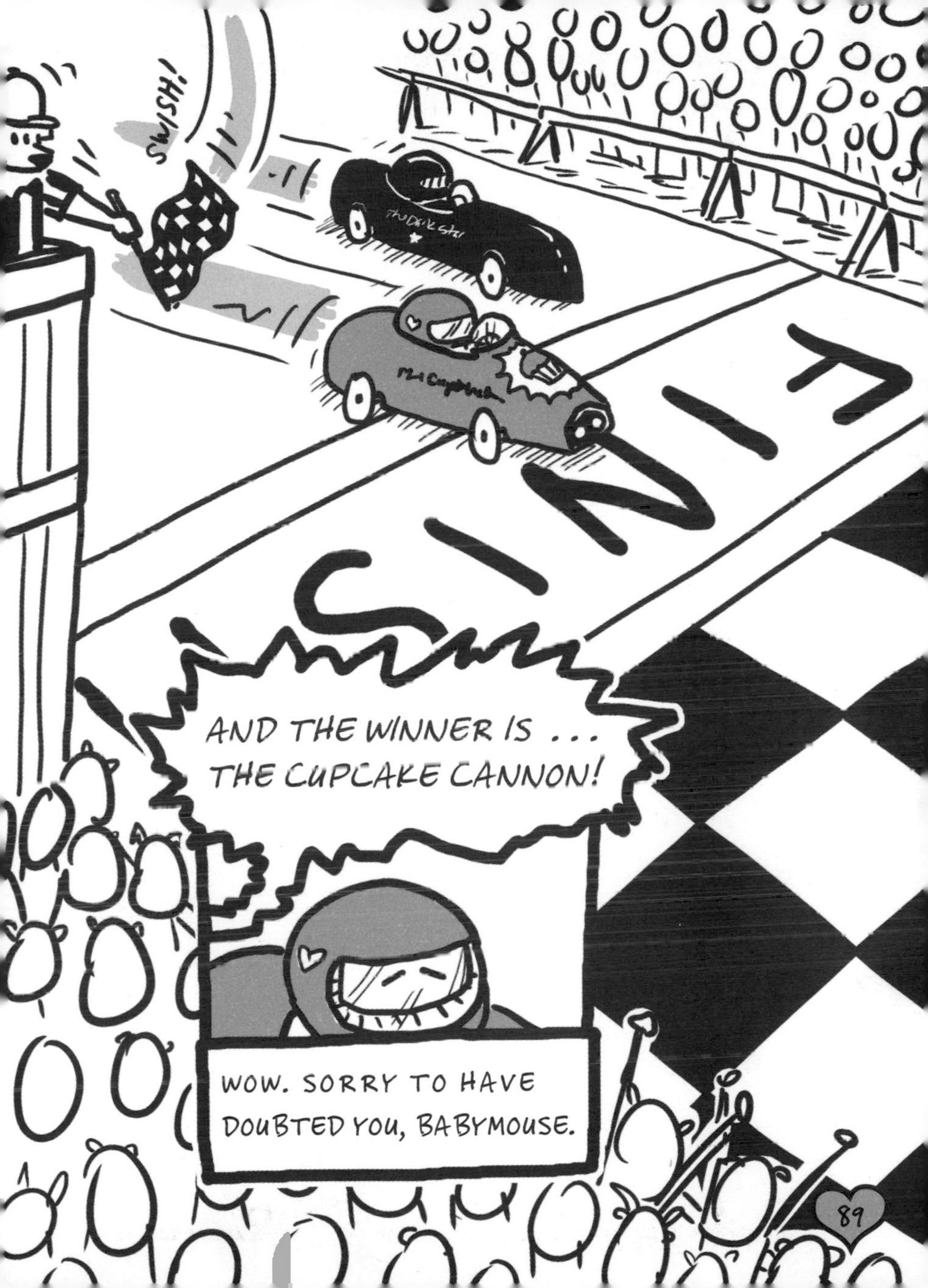
SWISH!
FINISH
AND THE WINNER IS . . .
THE CUPCAKE CANNON!
WOW. SORRY TO HAVE
DOUBTED YOU, BABYMOUSE.

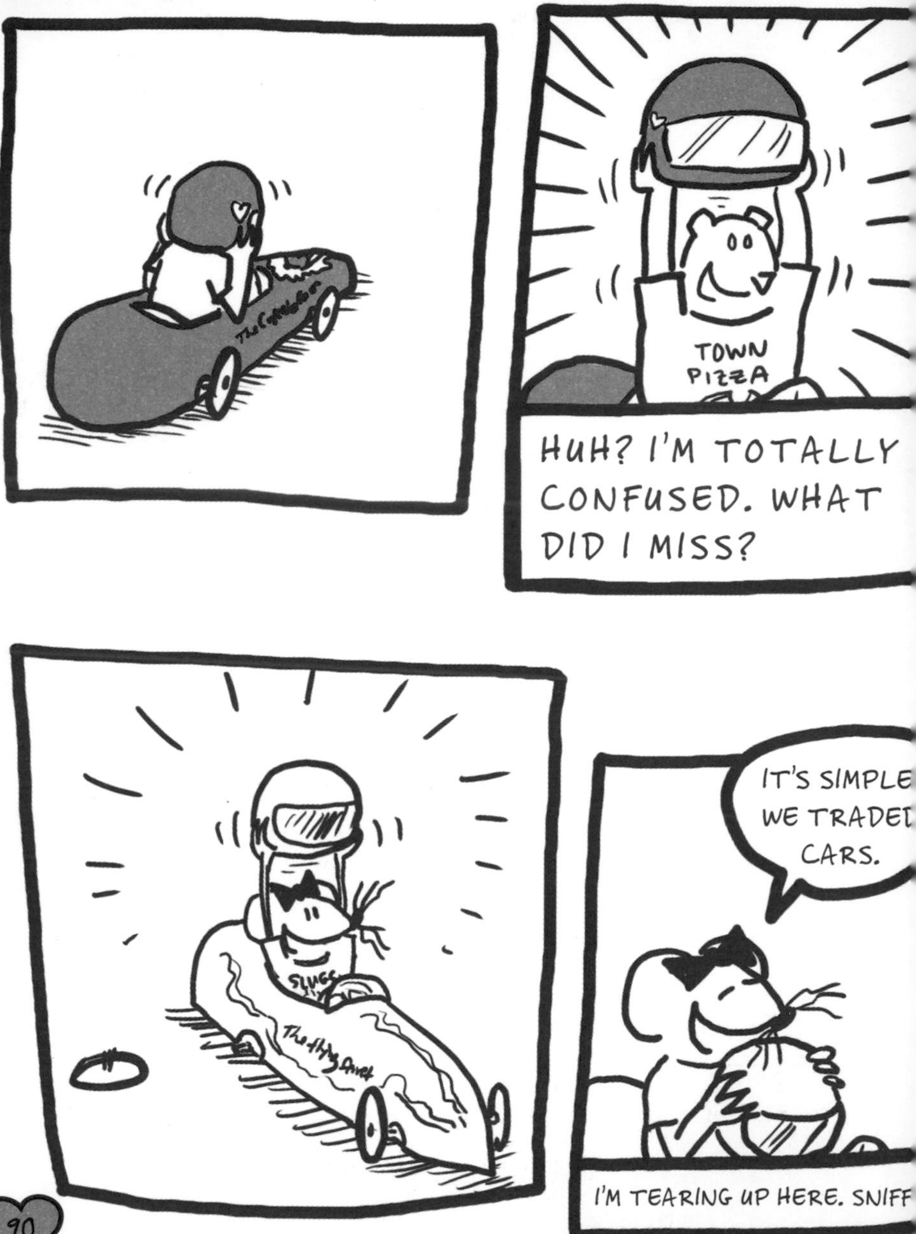
TOWN
PIZZA
HUH? I'M TOTALLY CONFUSED. WHAT DID I MISS?
IT'S SIMPLE WE TRADED CARS.
I'M TEARING UP HERE. SNIFF

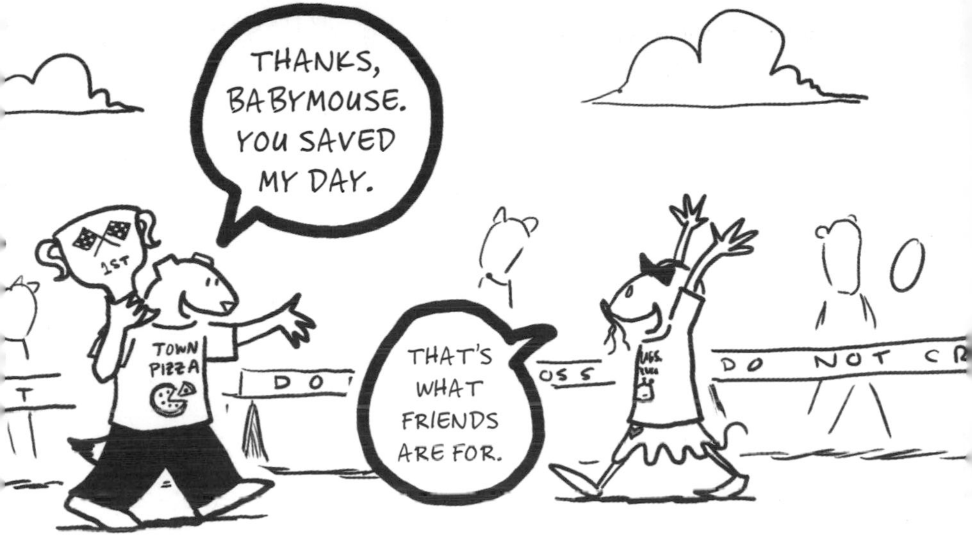
THANKS, BABYMOUSE. YOU SAVED MY DAY.
THAT'S WHAT FRIENDS ARE FOR.
TOWN PIZZA
1ST
DO NOT CR

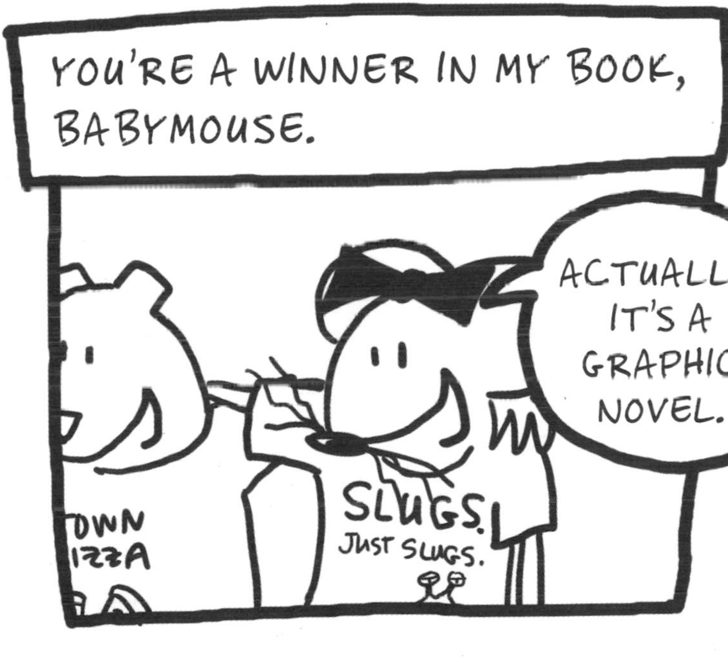
YOU'RE A WINNER IN MY BOOK, BABYMOUSE.
ACTUALLY, IT'S A GRAPHIC NOVEL.
SLUGS. JUST SLUGS.

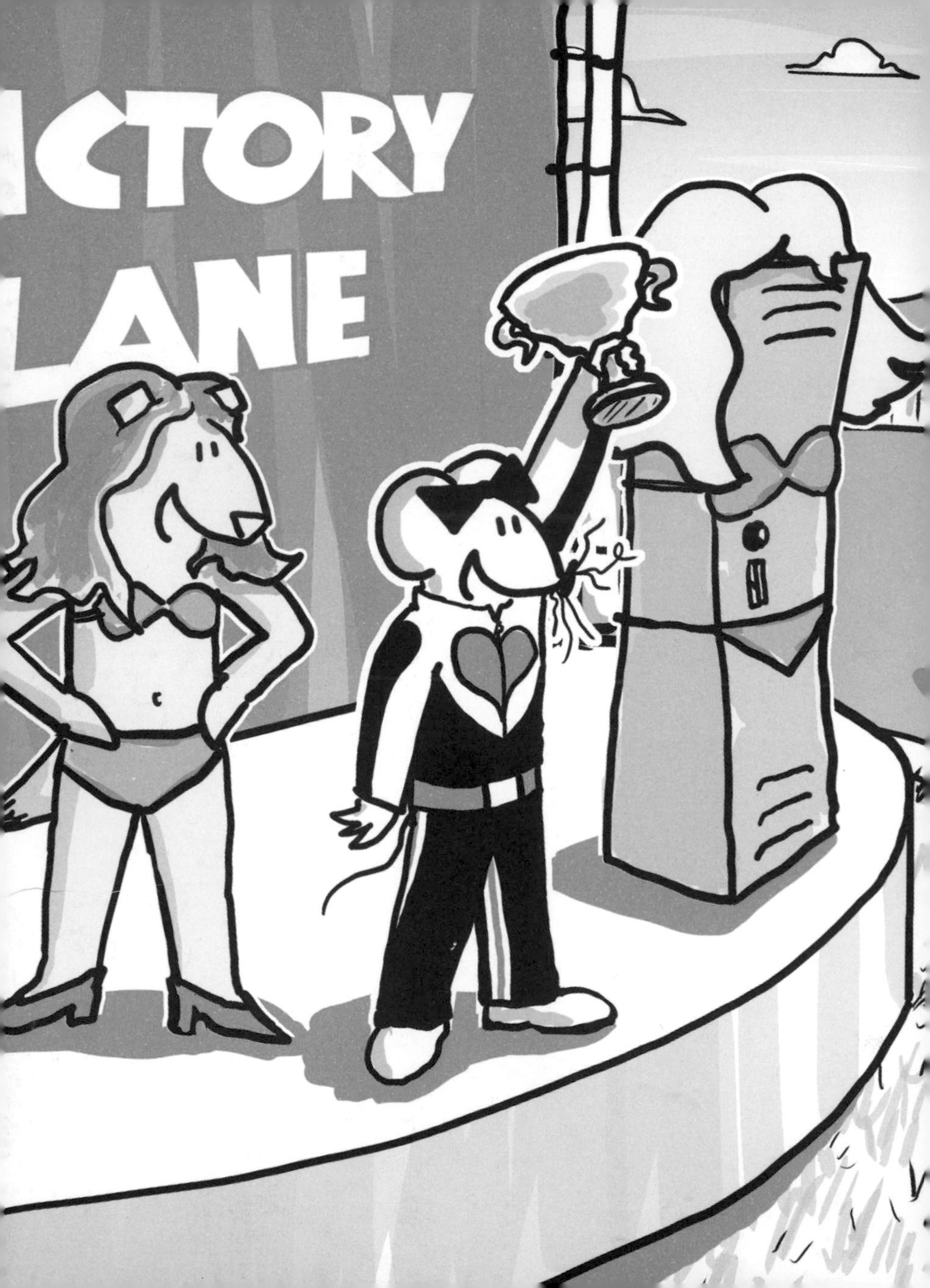
ICTORY
LANE

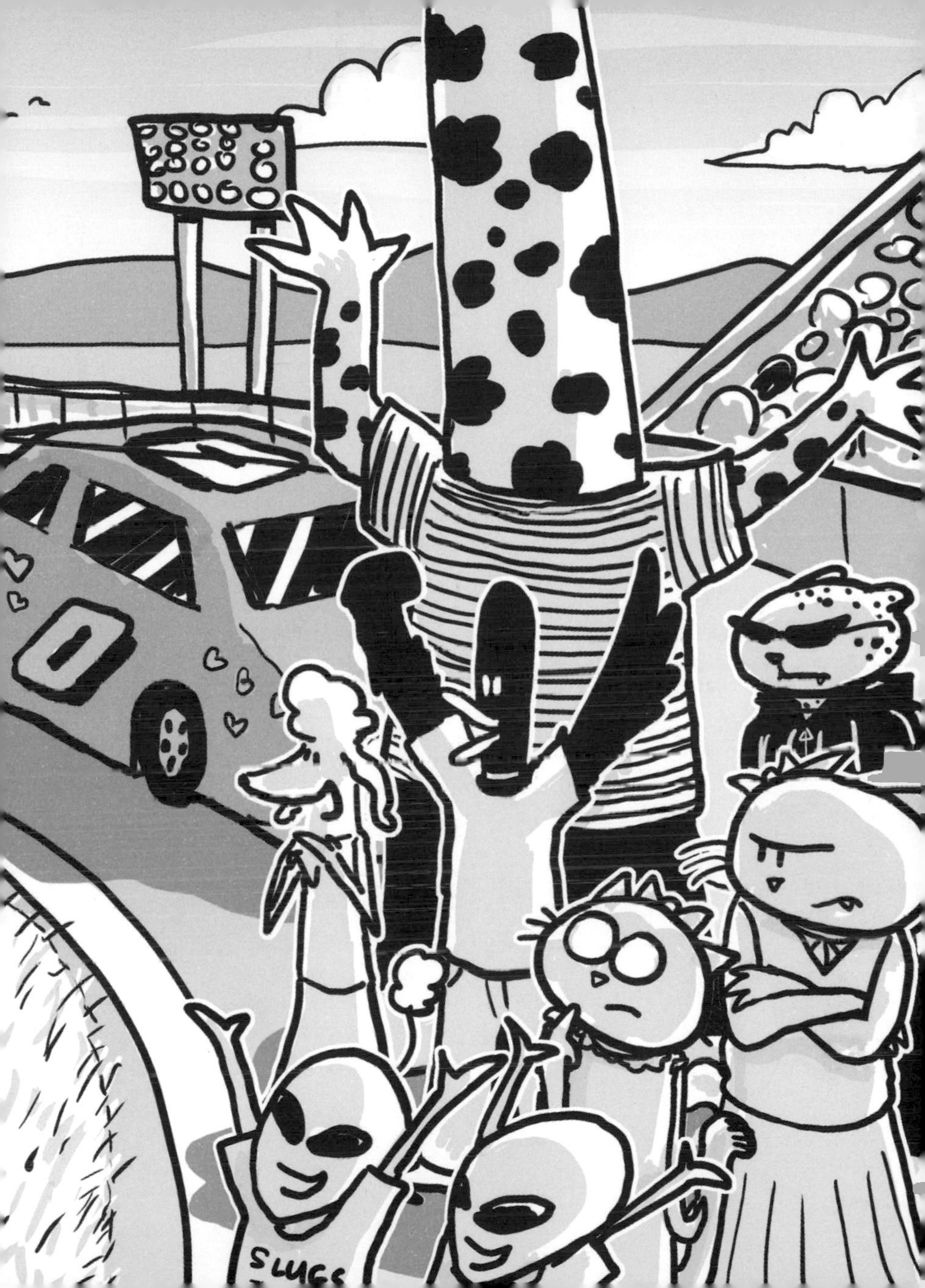
SLUGS

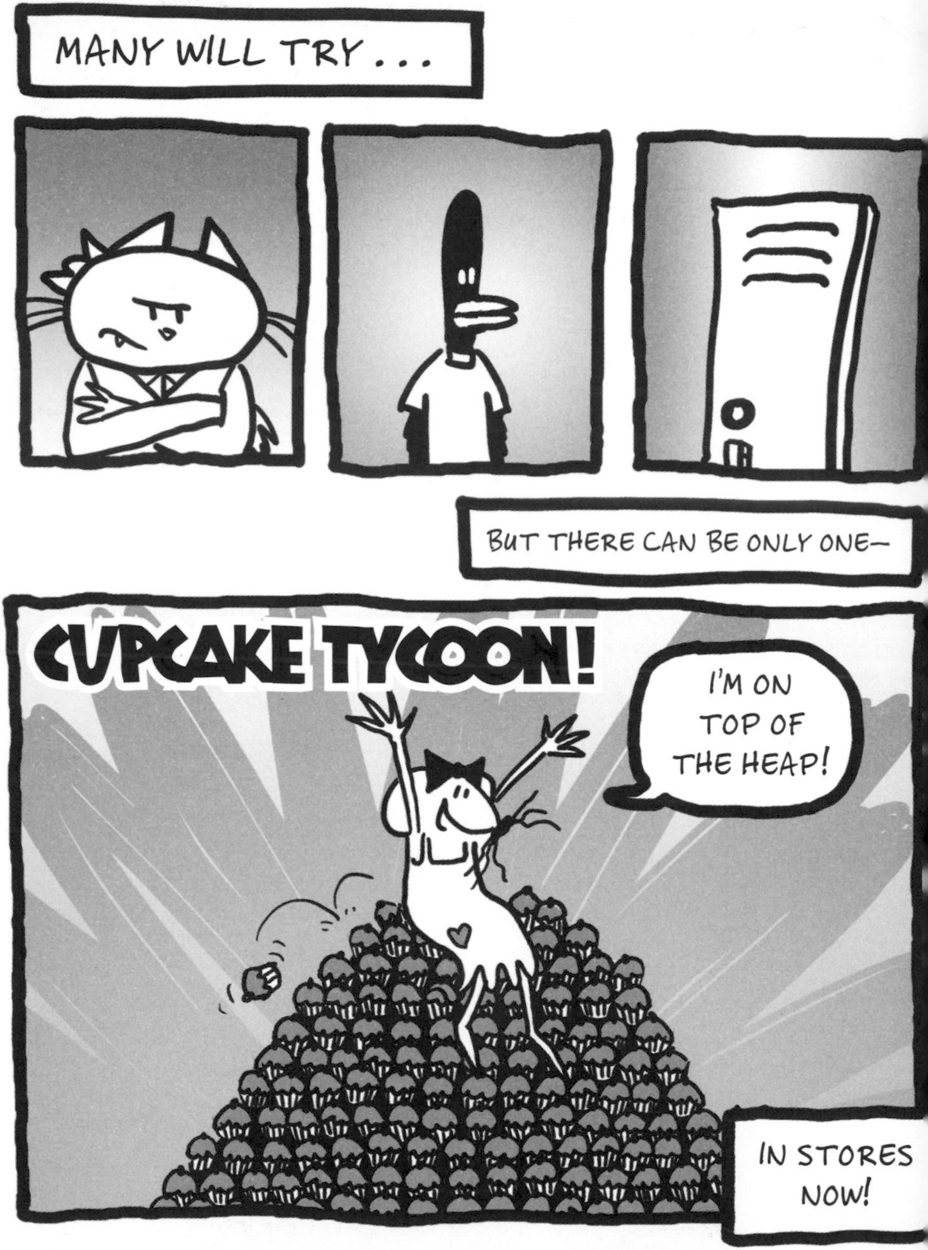
MANY WILL TRY . . .
BUT THERE CAN BE ONLY ONE—
CUPCAKE TYCOON!
I'M ON TOP OF THE HEAP!
IN STORES NOW!

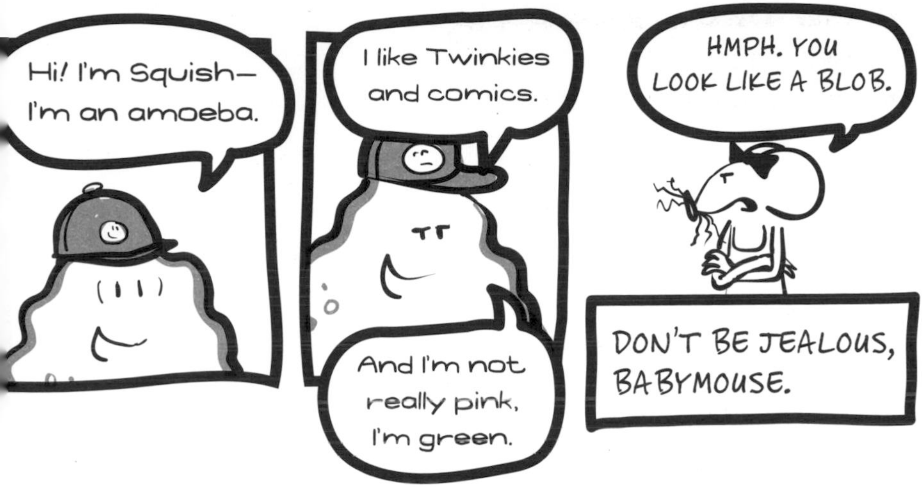
Hi! I'm Squish—
I'm an amoeba.
I like Twinkies
and comics.
And I'm not
really pink,
I'm green.
HMPH. YOU
LOOK LIKE A BLOB.
DON'T BE JEALOUS,
BABYMOUSE.

READ ABOUT SQUISH'S AMAZING ADVENTURES IN:

#1 SQUISH: Super Amoeba

#2 SQUISH: Brave New Pond

#3 SQUISH: The Power of the Parasite

#4 SQUISH: Captain Disaster

#5 SQUISH: Game On!

#6 SQUISH: Fear the Amoeba

AND COMING SOON:

#7 SQUISH: Deadly Disease of Doom

★ "IF EVER A NEW SERIES DESERVED TO GO VIRAL, THIS ONE DOES."
—*KIRKUS REVIEWS*, STARRED